# Roth-Steyr

First published in Great Britain in 2020 by Black Shuck Books

This edition © Black Shuck Books 2022
All content © Simon Bestwick 2022

Cover design by WHITEspace
Set in Caslon by WHITEspace
www.white-space.uk

978-1-913038-57-1

# Roth-Steyr

by
Simon Bestwick

BLACK
SHUCK
BOOKS

*For Gary McMahon,*
*From one Hood Man to another*

In so many ways, I'm used to the cold. A positive advantage in my job: the mortuary's always freezing. You often say you don't know how I stand it. But it's easy enough.

It isn't for everybody, and not the role I envisaged for myself, but I'm good at it. Thorough, diligent; that still means something. I joined so I could be of use; even if the people who come in here are beyond all human aid, I can give them some dignity, and with luck answer their loved ones' questions of how and why they died. And I can lay them out so that when those loved ones come to identify them, it's no more painful or traumatic than it has to be.

There are four of us standing around one of the mortuary slabs tonight. Five, if you count the gentleman lying prone before us with his Y-incision crusted black with stitches and his twice-ventilated skull. There's my boss, Dr Sharma, and Detective Inspector Reeve, a stocky man who's run to fat late in life. A heavy gut, stubbly jowls and tangled black hair; before the flab set in I can picture him as the terror of a rugby league pitch in darkest Yorkshire. He takes that kind of approach to his work, bulling head-down through all barriers, not giving up until he gets there. He reminds me of someone, although I can't place who. Someone from long, long ago, I expect. So many people *that* could be.

"No ID," Reeve's saying. "No scars or tattoos. No distinguishing marks."

"I know," says Dr Sharma. "There's normally *something*. You're running his prints?"

Reeve nods. "What about DNA?"

"Waiting to see if he's in the database. Won't get anywhere with dentals. His teeth are perfect."

They won't get anywhere with fingerprints or DNA, either. He'll lie in a freezer drawer, bullet holes plugged with wax, until they run out of room or patience and send him off to the crematorium. Ashes to ashes. The freezer will keep decomposition at bay till then, but his long-delayed return – dust to dust and earth to earth – is underway.

I feel a sharp pang, sharper than I've felt anything for a while, except when I'm with you. Nothing else touches me, but this does. I could tell them his name, what to put on his stone. But I don't, can't. I can't even squeeze his dead hand or kiss his cold brow, for fear of inviting comment. I want to tell him that I'm sorry, but I can't. And one day I'll be like him.

"Mr Veale?" says Reeve.

The last member of our little conclave is a small, plump man, balding and bespectacled, with the rumpled look of one who lives alone. Like every ballistics expert I've ever met, he's an odd duck, which might explain the living-alone part. He asked me out to dinner once, red-faced and stumbling with embarrassment; I let him down gently, telling him about you and that I was exclusively interested in women. He was a perfect gentleman about it, and we've remained on good terms ever since. Men of the twenty-first century take note: many of you could learn something from Mr Veale.

"There might be a useful lead," he says. Mr Veale's voice tends to hoarseness, but it's strong and confident, even though he can't quite manage to look anyone in the eye. "We recovered a spent cartridge from the crime scene. It's an unusual weapon."

Of course it was. It's the ammunition, not the gun, that counts, but so many of us are traditionalists in our choice of weapons, maintaining that last link with who we were.

"An 8mm Roth-Steyr," says Mr Veale, and I close my eyes.

———

At least today's a short shift. We've planned a date night; a meal together, then back home so that I can undress you slowly by candlelight and rub scented oils into your naked back.

We've been together three years, and these nights matter: little oases of self-created joy. And I want to make love to you, but all I can hear is Mr Veale's hoarse voice, saying *Roth-Steyr, Roth-Steyr, Roth-Steyr*, over and over again.

And so my fingers glide over your skin and I want to sink into you, lost in tactile sensation, so that I can't tell where I end and you begin, but it's not happening. You can feel it too; you turn onto your back. Your breasts are golden in the candlelight.

You light it all up. Everything. You add colour and taste, aroma and song. You're velvet and silk, a kiss on my lips, a tongue teasing my clit from its hood. Nothing else touches me as you do: moth-like I flit from light to light and love to love, but you burn brightest of all.

"What's wrong?" you say.

"Nothing," I lie.

"Valerie." You only use my full name when annoyed. "Come on."

"It's nothing," I lie again. "Nothing to do with you." True, at least. "Just work." A half-truth there.

Your hand slides up my arm. "Bad one?"

"Reminded me of someone." And so I tell you about a girlfriend's brother who died in a car wreck when I was still at school, and how a body on the slab today reminded me of him. I hate lying to you, hate it. But what good would the truth do either of us, even if you believed me? You give everything, and in return I offer all I can, but it's not enough, and I can't even tell you how you've been shortchanged. This isn't what love should be, but it's all that I can have and all that I can offer.

I want to tell you about my childhood; my *real* childhood, not the tales I've told you of a suburban girlhood in the North-East. I want to tell you my real name: not Valerie Varden, but the *Gräfin* Valerie Elisabeth Franzsiska von Bradenstein-Vršovci. A Countess, no less, or at least I was, until the Austrian nobility were abolished in 1918.

I want to tell you about the family palace at Bradenstein. About the lake beside the house; how Ulrich and I would row out to the island in the middle to proclaim ourselves its King and Queen (though still loyal to the Emperor, of course). I'd tell you how one winter Ulrich fell through the ice on the lake, and that I saved him. I'd tell you about the black and gold carriage with the family crest, how the footmen would race down the steps to meet it. About my maid, Katrin, plump and soft-skinned, with her deep breasts, wide hips, blue eyes, black hair, how she was the first girl I fell in love with, the first I kissed. I want to tell you about the first girl I made love with; she called herself Paulina, but I'll never know her real name. I want to tell you about growing up in the opulent twilight of an Empire, about old Vienna and Budapest and Prague, about the clenched horror in my stomach when I heard that the Archduke had been killed in Sarajevo; about the leaden, tumorous dread that horror became, and how it thickened and grew through the July Crisis. How, when they finally arrived, the first declarations of war – and the rest that followed, dragging Europe into cataclysm nation by nation, alliance by alliance, like so many weights on a chain – came as a relief.

On the way to the hospital, I stop at the Catholic Church and, although I no longer believe, I light a candle for Erick.

Something else I longed to tell you last night – that his name was Erick von Kulmer, that I danced with him at my 21$^{st}$ birthday ball in 1910. A friend of Ulrich's, tall and wide-shouldered, magnificent in his dress uniform. I couldn't, of course, any more than I could tell DI Reeve, Dr Sharma or Mr Veale. Erick will be buried nameless and unclaimed.

Ulrich, Erick and I. And Tibor, of course. Who else is left? Albin died in Lisbon in 1943, though not without mortally wounding his quarry. Cold comfort all the same. Stefan and Mathias walked into a trap in Istanbul in 1927 and were each shot neatly in the back of the head: Janacek's work, we heard. As far as I know, other than myself, only Tibor and Ulrich now remain.

Erick came with me to Vienna in 1932. Ulrich wouldn't – he insisted our mission took priority, although in truth I think he didn't want to see what the city had become.

Vienna was barely recognisable. The First Austrian Republic was in its death throes, racked by inflation and paramilitary clashes on the streets. Within two years parliament would be abolished and the Fatherland Front in power, by way of a – thankfully brief – civil war. We soon left Vienna; I steeled myself and drove with Erick to Bradenstein.

By then, so tiny and truncated had Austria become, my childhood home lay across the Czechoslovakian border. The estate had been renamed Brada Kámen – a very rough attempt to 'Czechify' the name – and was long-abandoned. Ulrich and I had been the last of our parents' children: Conrad and Franz died in the Italian Alps in the 'White War', and Rolf's U-boat disappeared in the Adriatic in '17. After we walked the Sindelar Gate, we were officially listed as dead. My mother, never in the best of health, died two months later.

Three days after the funeral, Papa went to his study, wrote a short note on cream-coloured notepaper bearing the family crest, then put the barrel of his service revolver in his mouth and fired. He'd delayed his exit solely to ensure that all his affairs were settled and all arrangements made. Methodical to the last: prepare and plan, he'd used to say, and never act without considering the consequences.

Did he kill himself out of grief, or because he realised that our house was now to all intents and purposes extinct anyway, and his continued existence pointless? In either case, it's another burden to carry: I'd never paused to consider how our absence would be explained to our families. I'd assumed they'd have been told we were engaged in top secret work for the Empire, but someone must have thought it kinder to declare us dead than to torture our loved ones with false hope of a return. Parricide by proxy, as an unintended consequence of immortality.

The house, unclaimed, had fallen into ruin. A fire had completely destroyed the east wing and gutted much of the main building. Ivy and creepers had crawled over the blackened walls, as if covering the house's shame.

The gardens had grown wild, weeds and slime choking fountain and pond. The steps at the front of the house were broken and cracked, weeds and moss sprouting between the paving slabs. Every childhood memory blighted; my past burned and scoured away.

My past is gone, but will never leave me: ironic for someone with an endless future ahead. Ninety years and twelve hundred miles away from it (I've been British so long that I think in Imperial measurements now), Bradenstein is with me still. When I get to work, the bright-lit hospital corridors seem poised constantly to shift into the fire-blackened, rain-ruined ones of the old house; the stench of charred, rotten wood seeps up through the hospital's antiseptic smell.

I had to see it all, so I went inside, despite Erick's protests about the unsafe structure. That made me laugh – what did either of us have to fear from falls? Only one thing could kill us, and it wouldn't be found in there. Having removed myself from the chase, I tell myself I'm unlikely ever to be at risk from it now.

Although Erick's corpse – in my adopted city, my hospital, my mortuary – is an unsettling coincidence, if coincidence it is. And a reminder. Memento mori...

How many of us are left? How many people, in all, came through the Sindelar Gate alive? Fifty? Perhaps not even as many as that. And the Gate was destroyed, to prevent its capture. Talk about a dog in the manger attitude: here are the means of immortality – who knows what promise the future of mankind might offer with it? But our nation can't keep hold of it – so deny it to the world!

But maybe that shows the world's better spared such a gift. Why prolong our existences if that's all we make of them? After all, who did they send through the Gate? Artists? Philosophers? Scientists or poets? Musicians? Healers? No: greedy, violent men, lost in dreams of blood and gold... and people like me.

How many of us left, and how did the dead ones die? Oh, the cause of death would always be the same, of course: we've no other way *to* die. But whose trigger, and whose gun? Do we all reach a point at last where so much is gone that the loss becomes unbearable?

I only know my own answer to that, which is: *not yet*. I have purpose, at least for now; for now, at least, I make life work for me. Both the Black Eagles and the *Falkenjaeger* passed through the Sindelar Gate in 1918; as immortals, we're all young. Although we're still young and strong in body and limb, we've only just outstripped the outer limits of ordinary human longevity.

It's not a train of thought I relish; I'm glad to change into my uniform and make my way to the mortuary. I occupy myself with the night shift's leavings. An RTA victim who died on the table; an old woman who passed away in her sleep last night. I take the first one's fingerprints – the crash left him too mangled to be identified yet – then extract and spin blood samples from both bodies. I check inventory, place orders, inspect and clean the equipment. I keep my back to Erick's drawer throughout, trying not to feel its cold pressure at my back.

I wish Tibor was here. Tibor was one of the funniest men I've ever known – passionate, hot-hearted, witty, kind. I can see him now – short and rolly, with curly red hair and bristling mutton chops which he claimed to have grown in imitation of the Emperor (shaven off years before our last parting, but even so I can't picture him now without them.) Tibor's the one I miss the most. Ulrich and I used to be close, but we were strangers long before we parted ways in the rubble of Berlin.

You would have loved Tibor. If he's still out there, I wonder if there's a way to reach him: I know you want us to get married, and if we ever did I'd love him to walk me down the aisle. I wonder if he's married. Unlikely. Too many of us struggled with long-term relationships – what does that even mean, after all, for people like us? Small wonder then that all of the others – apart from Ulrich, and once or twice I wondered about him, since the normal rules of human existence hardly applied to us now – pursued me in the hope of an immortal bedmate. Or to see what progeny, miraculous or monstrous, I might give them. At least with Tibor, I knew I didn't have to worry: he was strictly interested in boys, as I was in girls. I so wish you could meet him. I so wish I could tell you who he really is. I so wish I could tell you who *I* really am, and didn't have to filter the truth through acceptable layers to give you what I hope you want.

But I left Tibor in the end; left all of them, and have seen and heard nothing since. There were channels we could still have used – and I checked them from time to time, in the hope of hearing from him – but there was only silence. They'd all chosen to shun me; perhaps they hoped that cutting me off from my kind might force me to return, that lone immortality among the ephemerals of the unaltered human race would become too much to bear, but it hasn't. So far.

The day passes. A long shift this time, but at last the end's in sight. Looks as though I might get away on time; we've nothing planned, but the two of us curled up like cats on the sofa in front of some Netflix show or other will be more than enough. Raging passion and rampant sex are all very well when you're seventeen, but for the long haul what matters is someone you can sit with, warm, in silence. You told me that, or something very like it, and I realised you were right: it was something I'd known for a long time but never put into words.

"Got one, Val," calls Dr Sharma. "'Fraid I'll need you to stick around."

"What have we got?" I say as the gurney wheels in, trying not to think of you beside me on the sofa, not to feel resentment; to remember, late though the hour is, that this is what I do, this is how I find meaning now. *Ich dien*: I serve.

"Unidentified white male, thirties. Gunshot wound to the head."

"Another one?" But then, I work in an inner-city hospital; gunshot wounds and stabbings are, sad to say, all part of life's rich tapestry hereabouts. Even so: "What is it, a full moon?"

"No idea," says Dr Sharma. "Reeve's on his way, though."

"Reeve? How come?"

"Might be linked to the one from yesterday."

"The Roth-Steyr?"

"That's the one. The weird gun. I was just trying to remember the name."

"Not an easy one to forget." But then, I already knew it. The Roth-Steyr, aka *Repetierpistole M.7*: adopted by the Austro-Hungarian cavalry in 1907, the first automatic pistol officially adopted by a major world power. Oh, I could give Dr Sharma chapter and verse on it; I know it intimately. An old weapon, and odd-looking to modern eyes, but it remains effective, accurate, and – above all – reliable, which is why they still turn up over a century later and, more to the point, still work.

Definitely not, however, your average Saturday night special. Glocks and Brownings practically grow on trees around here, and even a Kalashnikov will, if you know the right people, only set you back a couple of hundred pounds on the streets of Manchester, or so I am reliably informed. Antique cavalry pistols of the Habsburg Monarchy that fire a cartridge no other pistol in the world has ever used are, to put it mildly, not your average backstreet dealer's stock-in-trade.

"Yeah, but I managed." Dr Sharma grins. She has silvered black hair and a warm, friendly face, quick to smile; too much so, sometimes, since cheer and bonhomie aren't generally what the newly bereft have come here for. "Anyway, he's on his way, and so's your bit on the side Mr Veale."

"Mr Veale," I say primly, "is *not* my bit on the side."

"Hey, I don't judge. Anyway, let's try to get the bullets out so your boyfriend can do his magic."

She really isn't as funny as she thinks, but I don't rise to the bait. Instead I scrub and glove up, then fumble, numb-fingered, at the bodybag zip.

Let it be Varga, or Janacek. Any of them – God (what God?) knows there's been killing enough, but if the unending war or vendetta – whatever it is now – has claimed another life, let it be one of theirs, not ours. I even hope – and I know how appalled you'd be if I could only tell you a fraction of the truth, if I could even tell you that I had a brother, let alone a twin – that it will be Ulrich's face I see. But I know, even as I tug the zipper stiffly down, whose face I will find.

He's grown his mutton chops back. Everything comes back into fashion sooner or later – or, at the very least, becomes a hipster pose. His round kind face and big green eyes, his curly, coppery hair, are all unchanged by the passing of three-quarters of a century, except for the two black holes in his forehead, small and neat. When I turn his head to study the back of his skull there are no exit wounds. The bullets are still lodged inside. Mr Veale will find nothing of note about them, other than the unusual calibre: the rituals that made them so deadly to Tibor will have left them physically unaltered.

Mr Veale arrives. "Miss Varden," he says, all puppy dog eyes and nervous smile.

"Mr Veale," He doesn't need to be here; I already know the gun will be the same, and so will the killer. But I just smile back. Keep up appearances at all costs: I've learned to be good at that.

I help Dr Sharma extract the bullets and Mr Veale grins like a schoolboy, then races for the door in search of his lab, almost knocking over Inspector Reeve as he goes.

Reeve approaches, looking down at Tibor. "Recognise him?"

I start. "What? No."

"Sorry." He's still watching me. "Just looked as though you did."

Shit. "No," I lie, "nothing like that. He just reminded me of someone I knew."

Reeve studies me in silence for several seconds that feel a great deal longer, then nods slowly and looks down at the body. I find something to busy myself with; the last thing I need is Reeve thinking that I have something to hide. Because, of course, I do.

---

They're all gone now, then; all of them, except for Ulrich and I. And what would Ulrich do if we met again?

I know what I would do. *Do you remember the ice, Ulrich?* I would ask. *On the lake at Bradenstein, in the winter of '03? We were warned it wasn't strong enough but we wouldn't be told, so we took our skates and went out on it. But the ice was thin, little more than a rime, and as you skated across the lake it gave way under you and you plunged in, screaming. I was terrified for you, but I couldn't let myself rush out there, because the same thing would happen to me. Instead I crawled across the ice as you screamed and thrashed in the freezing water, praying as I went that you wouldn't drown before I could reach you. I was afraid of losing you, yes, but afraid, too, of how Papa and Mama would blame me if you died, of the shame and terrible bitterness that would haunt the house, of the guilt I'd always feel if harm came to you.*

*You didn't drown, of course, and I hauled you back onto the ice. Papa raged and shouted at us and Mama cried and screamed, and we cried too but we were all glad. Katrin the maid wrapped us in blankets by the fire and brought us hot chocolate; she held me to her deep soft lovely breasts as I cried. I'd been in love with Katrin, as children fall in love, long before that day, but that was the first moment that I felt what I would later recognise as sexual desire.*

One day I want to ask him this. To see if there's still some connection to be made, across the gap the years have opened, that's divided us completely since Berlin.

---

Normally whatever I've seen in my working day goes back in its box at shift's end and doesn't come home. But not tonight, and of course you spot that, because how could you not?

"What's wrong?"

"Nothing." I both hate and kick myself for saying that; the first because it's a lie and I don't tell you any more of those than I can help, the second because it isn't even a good or believable one.

"Hey." You move round the kitchen table to stand behind me, hands settling on my shoulders. They begin to gently squeeze and release. Massage; so often the overture to a night's lovemaking, but the only appetite currently on my mind is the one I'm gratifying with your homemade lasagne, although that could easily change once my plate's clean. In the meantime, it's soothing some of the tension from my muscles. Only some, not all: I can't make Tibor's face disappear. Or Erick's. Will Ulrich's be next? Or will it be one I might just about recognise from the files they showed us at Aehrenbach?

"Come on, Val, you can tell me."

I wish I could. "I just got a nasty shock today."

"Oh?" Your arms encircle me from behind.

We couldn't be more different. Me: tall and pale, long legs and narrow waist, a sharp, fine-boned face. Blue eyes and a fall of titian hair. You: small and rounded. Olive skin and black hair. Deep breasts I love to pillow my head upon, plump thighs you love to guide my mouth between, wide black eyes magnified to hugeness by your glasses. I'm a thing of lines and angles; you're one of softness and curves.

"Nothing bad," I say. "I mean, nothing *really* bad. We got another body that I thought I recognised."

"Again? Jesus!" You hold me tighter. "Who?"

"A friend from college." I take your hand and squeeze it. "It's okay. It wasn't him. Just looked a bit like him. Shook me up."

"Babe, I'm starting to get worried now."

"It's okay."

"That's twice this has happened."

"True."

"Maybe you've been working there too long. You should think about a change."

"Maybe." As soon as I've addressed the more pressing concern of my survival.

"I mean it. You're good with people. You're wasted there."

"I deal with the families." I don't want to talk about this. I don't have the energy.

"It's still a waste. You could retrain like I did. You'd be a good counsellor."

"Maybe." I just want you to drop the subject now. You seem to pick up on that; instead of saying anything else you kiss the top of my head. Your hands move to my upper arms, fingertips circling gently over my skin through the thin blouse. I love your touch, and my body responds to it. You're wonderful to me, and deserve so much, and I offer so little in return.

I can't shake off an ever-growing sense of doom. Something's coming, I'm sure, has been for a while. A vague, intermittent but deep unease has troubled me over the past couple of months, but it's become far more focused and intense since Erick turned up on my slab last night. The life I've led as Valerie Varden has been the happiest I've had in years, and the last three have been best of all. I should have known: life is cruel. It lets you taste the sweetness, then strikes the cup from your lips.

With Tibor dead as well, there's no denying the threat. The war has come here. Will it be Janacek who comes for me, or Varga? Am I the next target, or is it Ulrich? Is he already lying dead and unclaimed, somewhere in this city? Or did he fall in some other battle, long ago?

I don't want to think, not now. At least you're making that part easier for me. I turn my head; I kiss your mouth. "Upstairs?" you say.

I nod, and for a while the past and the future, both equally full of darkness, disappear. Instead there's only a present filled with sensation, warmth and laughter.

And I wish, again and again, that I could tell you. Because the right thing to do, the clever, sensible thing, if I truly love you and rate your happiness and safety above my own, is to leave. No explanations, no goodbyes – because I can't tell you the truth. And so I have no way to prevent you hating me. But I should be willing to suffer that, shouldn't I?

I kiss your warm belly and lay my head there, close my eyes as you stroke my hair.

Where do things begin? It's so hard to pinpoint the moment, even something this simple and perfect.

Perhaps it was in the hospital staffroom where you almost tripped over my outstretched legs as I caught a few minutes' much-needed sleep in a chair. Back when I was a nurse, before I retrained and transferred to the comparative peace of the mortuary (even immortals have limits to how much pain they can witness). We were both nurses then, although you were already planning to become a counsellor, to specialise in victims of domestic violence.

The urge to help, the need to serve. I recognised and admired that, but was that where love began? We started talking then, but were we anything more than colleagues at that point; could you have even called it friendship?

Was it when I realised that when I went to the break room, or anywhere near your department, that I was hoping you'd be there? When I realised I was inventing or looking for reasons to cross your path? When did you realise you were doing that? We never really compared notes to see if it happened for us at the same time.

"Ow," you mumble, pushing lightly at my head. I move to lie alongside you, face to face. You give me a drowsy kiss then turn away, onto your side. I draw the covers, which fell to the floor while we fucked, over us, and mould myself against your back.

"Little spoon," you giggle as you sink into sleep. I cradle you tight, kissing your hair. Is it touched with grey? Three years isn't really long enough for it to be apparent to you that I haven't aged. But, thirty, forty, a hundred years from now, I'll always look the same. We can never grow old together.

I could never pinpoint exactly when we first became close, much less when our friendship became something else (a shock to you as you'd only ever been with men before; I'm that rarity among lovers who can honestly say she's reached her beloved in ways she'd never been reached before, or thought she could be); similarly, if I try to trace the chain of events that made me what I am, I get lost in endless causes and effects.

I was always, as they say today, gender non-conforming. Understand, though, that even though I wished aloud that I'd been born one on several occasions, I never truly wanted to be a boy. My body never felt anything but right to me: I never desired to trade my cunt for a cock. What I envied were the opportunities that I, as a woman, was expected to forego, that were any man's for the taking. Well, I was never the sort to dab my eyes with a lace handkerchief at the family fireside while the men marched off to fight.

Thankfully, the Habsburg Empire in its last decades was, beneath its veneer of strict manners and protocol, quite permissive if you knew where to go – although compared to present-day Britain, it was still positively draconian. Britain is more permissive still: too much so, I sometimes think, but perhaps that's just the old woman in me talking. Even passing through the Sindelar Gate can't guard against *every* change the years inflict.

But I should relish the licence while I can. If a century and a quarter of existence has shown me anything, it's impermanence. This too shall pass, whatever it may be. Don't you think that I took my world – with its hierarchies and traditions, its moral certainties, its politics and institutions – for granted too? Your morals, your certainties, will be gone one day as well, and sooner than you think. The pendulum is swinging back, to a long dark night of the European soul; perhaps the world's. Sooner or later, like the one I grew up in and so many others before and in between, this world too will fall.

And then there's the rest of the story; not my own beginnings but the wider picture beyond, the upheavals within the Empire itself. There were others before and others since but really, it began with Rudolf and Mary, in the year of my birth. It began with Mayerling.

Baroness Mary Vetsera, aged seventeen, wasn't the Crown Prince Rudolf's only mistress, but she would, ultimately, be the one who mattered. The course of history was altered by their deaths; it wasn't the final, or even the only, nail in the Habsburg coffin, but it was one of the most important. It's why I'm still alive; it's even how I got my name.

I know the story better than most historians, but I still wonder how exactly it began. When that first meeting, or rather that first moment of *connection* between them, took place. Some say they were together only three months, others that it was closer to three years. Did she know what he'd be to her, or he what she'd do to him? Was one smitten and the other all unknowing (and if so, which?) or was it mutual from the start?

I know how I've always pictured it, whether it's the truth or not. I picture Rudolf, lonely, melancholic, desperately unhappy, for all his wealth and privilege: he's resplendent in his white uniform, the Princess Stephanie on his arm, surrounded by servants and hangers-on and all the magnificent, stultifying pomp of Imperial senescence. I imagine him in the hall of some sumptuous palace, looking up at a landing overhead, to see her there. "Her full and triumphant beauty," Louise of Coburg wrote, "her cameo-like profile, her throat of a goddess, and her arresting sensual grace." Wavy dark hair piled atop her head, the deepest, blackest, most alluring eyes and some secret, indefinable quality that sets her apart from the rest. Even Rudolf can't give it a name, but he sees it, just as she sees something more than passing lust, and in that moment the connection is made and the future decided: the road to Mayerling, deep in the Vienna Woods. *Yes*, I imagine her saying with her eyes, answering the question in his: *Yes. You. I'll die with you.*

My shift the next day doesn't start till eleven a.m., but I lie: "They want me in early again," I call up the stairs. "Nine o'clock start."

"Oh for fuck sake." Steam billows across the landing and you appear at the top of the stairs, towelling your hair. You're in no rush this morning; your first client isn't until ten. "Tell them I'd like to see you occasionally."

I run upstairs and kiss you. Your skin's still damp from the shower. "See you later."

I don't want to leave. I have to. I don't want to leave you and never see you again. But I know I should.

I need to keep my options open. I get in the car and drive out of the suburb where we live, to the nature reserve nearby. I get out of the car and take a rucksack containing a collapsible shovel from the trunk.

This time of the morning, on a weekday, the reserve is quiet. These are the kinds of times that I like to come to places like this. We both do. It's one of the many things we have in common.

The nature reserve is dotted with ruins and scattered bricks. There was a landslide here in the 1920s, less than a decade after I walked the Gate. The boles of the trees have grown thicker than my own body since then; from seeds and shoots to this, while I'm unchanged. Ageless. Deathless.

Unless Janacek, or Varga, or whoever, gets me in the sights of his Roth-Steyr.

I'm looking for one landmark in particular: a brick wall about the height of my chest rising from a hillock beneath a looming oak. Below it are the foundations of a building, green with glossy ivy.

When I've found the spot I'm looking for, I pull the ivy aside, then take out the shovel and start to dig.

A dog starts barking, not far away, and I stop. I'm afraid, but not of the dog; I love dogs. It's the memories the barking brings back just now that I hate. And, more to the point, what if the dog walker's heading this way? What will I say if I'm seen?

The shovel blade hits metal. I scrape the earth away. The biscuit tin is wrapped in an old carrier bag. With fingers and shovel blade, I prise it loose. Worms and woodlice fall back into the hole. Something heavy clunks against the inside of the tin.

The dog barks again, closer still. I stuff the box into the rucksack, collapse the shovel and pack that away too, cursing through my teeth as it snags on the lining as though conspiring to humiliate me. Concern for appearances: another value I was raised with, rejected in my youth but insistently returning as time marcheth on. At last it's all packed away and up the slope I go, the rucksack on my back, to perch on the wall beneath the oak, looking down at the river.

"Morning!" A sixtyish weather-tanned man waves from the footpath, a big Alsatian bounding in his wake. I wave back. "Lovely day."

"Certainly is!" I call back.

He strides off; the dog glances back at me before gambolling off as well. Almost as if he knows. When all's quiet, I climb down off the wall and walk back to the car.

---

I stop at a coffee shop, drink a caramel latte I don't really want, then shut myself in the disabled toilet. Now I have the space and privacy I need.

I open my backpack and unwrap the biscuit tin. I'm surprised how much my fingers shake. It's that bloody dog, reminding me.

The stiff plastic sheeting, caked with brittle mud, crackles when unwrapped, strewing dirt on the floor. The design on the biscuit tin has faded and the lid rusted almost solidly into place, but – muttering throughout under my breath and between my teeth, as if uttering an incantation – I work it loose.

Underneath are two bundles, wrapped in chamois leather. Inside the smaller one: a box of ammunition, the bullets caked in yellow protective grease, and a pair of stripper clips. The second heavier, bulkier one contains a crook-handle of black, glinting steel, shark-sleek and fatal. The curved grip, the wolflike snout of the barrel, the round-handled bolt at the rear.

It rolled off the production line at Fegyver- és Gépgyár in Csepel in 1907, eighteen years almost to the day after I was born, and it's worn the passage of a century and more almost as well as I have. It's been well-cared-for, and of course whole decades have passed without my so much as loading a bullet into the thing. Unlike people, guns can last almost forever given a little TLC and grease. Not that those things can't benefit a person, as we both know from certain date nights… but I digress.

I work quickly, cleaning off the excess grease. The pistol's action is smooth. At first, loading the stripper clips is awkward, fumbling work, but like riding a bicycle, it all comes back.

The first time I tried to load the stripper clips, my fingers bled. They were delicate, aristocratic fingers after all, more used to playing a piano. So said Sergeant Horváth, anyway, overlooking the fact that I was very unladylike and a better shot than any of my brothers. But I was used to heavy revolvers like my father's pistol, not these newer self-loaders.

"Come on, your ladyship, come on! Mama and Papa can't help you if you're too slow out there! Guns don't care about money and jewels, or who your family are! That's why I love them!"

Sándor Horváth had been in the army thirty years, essentially devoting his life to serving the Emperor, but hated the upper classes, apparently up to and including the level of royalty, with a passion that would have made Béla Kun look like Count Tisza. Did he survive the war, I wonder, and what role did he play in the Revolution or its suppression? I can equally well see him tearing down all that he once served, trading one set of certainties for another and giving his loathing full rein, or fighting to the last to save that old order; even if he detested its rulers, they were still *his*.

But at that point, I knew only that he was a man with the means and will to torment his social superiors with impunity. No coincidence, I expect, that he was considered one of the best trainers of officer-cadets in the Empire. Which was why he'd been given the task of training the *Falkenjaeger*.

My relationship with Sergeant Horváth played out at Aehrenbach, a wooded estate in the Salzkammergut not far from the Traunsee, and could most accurately be described as love-hate – until the very end, where the hatred, at least on my side, became absolute. The cause of which was the gun I'm currently reloading.

A stripper clip is a speedloading device that holds a number of cartridges – ten, in this case – to load a weapon more quickly and more easily. One by one, I fit bullets into both clips; doing so relaxes me.

Horváth was a petty tyrant, but at least he never treated me any differently from the rest. I was berated as savagely as any of the men, and when practising unarmed combat he never pulled his punches.

The Sergeant had seen a great deal of action and could kill not only with a rifle or pistol, but with a knife, rope, length of wire or his bare hands. His job was to pass those skills on to us.

"What's the point of this?" I remember Tibor demanding as he clambered wheezing to his feet, having been knocked flat by Horváth yet again. "None of this will be necessary."

"Will it not, fat boy?" grinned Horváth. He was hard and stocky and muscled despite his years. A granite block of a man. "You seem very sure."

"They can only be killed by the bullets." Tibor was reddening. "We can't choke them or break their necks."

For answer, Horváth unholstered his Steyr-Hahn pistol and pulled back the slide. It rang loud in the ballroom where we'd spent the last few weeks of our lives. Bare walls and floor, one corner partitioned into a sleeping area with hard iron-framed beds for the fifteen trainees in our group. Mattresses hard as bricks and thin linen sheets stiff as wood from starch. Everything at Aehrenbach was like that, all pomp and decoration stripped away to underline that here, our rank and wealth meant less than nothing and that the only realities were life and death, killers and killed, haters and hated. (What a Bulgarian poet I once knew would have called 'a world of ultimate reality'. He'd read far too much D'Annunzio, and taken him far too seriously, the poor lamb.) "No four poster beds for you here, Countess," Horváth would crow, "no featherbeds, no pillows full of down, no warming pan or servants to wipe your arse for you. *They* won't give two shits who your family are: they'll kill you or you'll kill them. Blue blood, red, it's all the same in the end."

Tibor took a step back, some of the redness leaving his face. The Sergeant wasn't pointing the gun at him, of course… but he wasn't *not* doing so, either.

Tibor was both tempted to apologise and furiously resistant to doing so; I could see the fear and pride fighting for possession of his face. I don't know what might have happened if Horváth had remained silent any longer. But then he shrugged. "No doubt you're right, Count Thököly," he said, managing as always to make the title sound like an insult, then tossed the Steyr-Hahn to Tibor, who scrambled to catch it. "Kill me."

"What?"

Horváth spread his arms. "Well, I'm obviously neither use nor ornament any more, am I? If I can't even grasp so elementary a concept as that?" He took a couple of easy, sauntering steps towards Tibor, and I wanted to scream a warning – but if I did Tibor might be distracted, and I knew what Horváth could do to him in the seconds his attention was elsewhere.

"I can't serve the Emperor if I'm that stupid, can I? Stupid. Mad. Senile." Horváth pirouetted on one heel, as perfectly as any ballerina. "You know what to do, don't you, fat boy? You don't need any details about fighting hand to hand. You just need to point, and fire. Not hard. But you'd better hurry up—" Horváth spun again "—because I'm getting closer."

Tibor took a step back, half-raising the Steyr-Hahn. The rest of us were still: if we interfered the consequences, for Tibor and the rest of us, might be even worse. "Stop there, Sergeant," he said, trying to sound commanding.

Horváth stepped closer, arms still spread. "What will you do if I don't? I *want* you to shoot me, you silly little cunt. Come on, *buzoralo*, pull the trigger—"

Tibor brought the gun up and for all I know actually might have fired, but he'd let Horváth come too close. It happened too quickly for me to follow, but there was a cry of pain and Tibor hit the floor with an ugly, sickening thud. He let out another cry, although it was much weaker – the wind had been driven out of him. He lay with Horváth's foot on his throat, his gun arm pulled up and twisted rigid by the grip of the Sergeant's left hand on his wrist – and with the Steyr-Hahn, grasped in Horváth's right hand, jammed against his temple.

I took a step towards them. "Let's not get too close, boys and girl," Horváth said very softly, his knuckle white on the pistol's trigger. "Well, looks like old Horváth's not quite so gaga after all, doesn't it, fat boy?"

Tibor glared up at him with gritted teeth. Horváth pushed the pistol barrel harder into his temple. "*Doesn't* it, fat boy?"

"Yes!" The word was tight and high, squeezed out. I tensed, ready to rush the Sergeant. "Don't, girly," he said, not even looking at me. "Looks like you're a silly little cunt who knows fuck-all, doesn't it, fat boy? Say 'Yes, Sarge'."

"Yes, Sarge."

"And if you can't shoot one old git who doesn't even have a gun, you're not much fucking use to His Imperial and Royal Apostolic Majesty, are you? Not much point wasting *you* on the Sindelar Gate. Eh? No," he said, before Tibor could respond, "so the best thing to do's what you should've done to me – *this!*"

Horváth pulled the trigger and I think all of us cried out, but the Steyr-Hahn only clicked. Tibor's scream became a whimper, then ragged panting breaths.

"Well," Horváth straightened up, "maybe I *do* need culling after all."

I went for him then, a fast cheetah run across the floor, and leapt. He spun at the last second and thrust out an arm fist-first. It caught me in the solar plexus and I hit the ground with a crash and a groan, too winded even to cry out.

My eyes were streaming, but I could see Horváth standing over me, raising the pistol. He pulled back the slide, and a brass bullet clattered to the floor beside me. Horváth repeated the procedure again and again, till the magazine was empty and the Steyr-Hahn's slide locked back.

"Well, look at that," he said. "I only went and loaded it with dummy bullets." He produced another stripper clip, shoved it into the open breech and pushed the bullets down with his thumb to click one by one into the magazine.

The empty clip clattered to the floor; the Steyr-Hahn's breech snapped shut. "These, though," Horváth said, "these are live."

With that he left the ballroom, considering the lesson well-learned.

And in the here and now I pull back the bolt by its round knurled handle and push a stripper clip into the open breech, then press down on the cartridges with my thumb. ("Make sure the bullets are facing *forwards*, your ladyship – don't want any accidents, do we?") And click, click, click: one by one they disappear into the gun, pressing the magazine spring down.

When the last one's gone, I slide the bolt forward and remember the day I used this gun for the first time.

I suppose I could have used it before: Horváth handed pistols out daily for shooting practice, and afterwards to fieldstrip: disassemble, reassemble, then disassemble and reassemble again so that we would know all their workings inside out, but he always took them back at the end. He did the same sometimes with rifles and machine-guns, but pistols were the priority: the assignment, by its nature, leant itself to close work, so we familiarised ourselves with handguns of every kind.

Years later, recalling those times, I composed a ditty:

*"Steyr–Mannlichers, Lugers,*
*Solid-frame Rast and Gassers.*
*Roth–Steyrs and Steyr–Hahns*
*And broomhandle Mausers.*
*Borchardts and Bergmanns and Colts and Brownings.*
*These are a few of my favourite things…"*

One day, we were summoned to the ballroom. There was no sign of Horváth but we stood in silence, as we'd been ordered to beforehand. The Sergeant had a preternatural ability to walk in the instant someone spoke, whether we'd been waiting a minute or half an hour, and then woe betide the offender. We were convinced that he must be watching through a spyhole, but could never work out where he hid.

That day we stood for almost a full hour before the door crashed wide and Horváth strode in. "Attention!" he barked, and paced round us, nodding. At last he backed away towards the door he'd entered through, gazing from face to face; I don't know what he was looking for, even now, but at last he saw it, and beckoned me.

When I drew level with him he turned towards me, arm extended, and for one awful moment I thought he meant to put it around my shoulders. Instead, he pointed towards the door. I walked to it at a straight steady pace, then hesitated. I hadn't been ordered to go through, after all, and Horváth enjoyed catch catching people in assumptions. Behind me, he sighed. "Go on through, Countess."

I did as I was told. The doorknob was a dull brass globe, tarnished and unadorned. My hand smelt of metal after touching it.

(Sitting in the coffee-shop toilet a century later, I release the pistol and sniff the palm of my right hand. It smells of brass and iron.)

I closed the door behind me. A flight of stone steps led downwards, lit by a bare electric bulb. At the foot of these was another door. The walls were stone, and glistened.

Behind the second door was a large basement, again lit by bare light bulbs. The walls and floor and ceiling were bare and made of grey-black stone that shone with damp. It was empty, except for four things.

The first object I saw was the largest – a plain wooden table, unvarnished and unadorned. On it was the second: a small flat cardboard box. The third object was a wicker basket on the floor, from which the fourth stared at me with large, dark eyes, rose up on small, slender legs and padded over.

He was a little grey terrier of some kind, floppy-eared, woolly-haired and about the height of my knee, with a fierce, affectionate little face: a far cry from the sleek hounds and waddling lapdogs I'd grown up with. He cocked his head to one side to study me, then sniffed my fingers and licked my hand. I couldn't resist crouching to pet him, listening out in case the door opened.

It didn't, however, and eventually I relaxed. Sooner or later Horváth would appear; most likely he was giving orders to the others. Left to myself I might have stood mutely at attention till he arrived, but the dog's presence made that impossible.

So I crouched and stroked him while he happily licked my face (the dog, not Sergeant Horváth: now *there's* an image I could gladly have made it to the heat death of the universe without.) I soon discovered he (the dog, again) particularly enjoyed having his chest rubbed, and being scratched behind the ears. Naturally, that was when Horváth arrived. Again, I can't shake off the suspicion that he might have been keeping watch, the better to judge the moment for his entrance.

I jumped to my feet, snapped to attention and waited. My face felt hot and I looked straight ahead. Felt a bead of sweat trickle from my short-cropped hair, sting the corner of my eye, then run on, down my cheek.

Horváth chuckled. "At ease."

The door clicked shut behind him and he paced the room. He didn't look directly at me; instead he studied the walls, the ceiling, the floor, the table and the box, which I'd completely forgotten about. After the weeks of training, with only Horváth and the others for company, the dog had claimed my full attention.

Besides, I'd been doing my best not to think of it: the box wasn't there by chance, and would have a part to play in whatever Horváth had in mind. But then, of course, so would the dog. Nothing was in that room by chance.

Still the Sergeant didn't look at me, but he did turn his attention to the dog. I have to admit that I flinched. Did he see? Oh, without a doubt: Sergeant Horváth never missed anything. He knelt and patted the dog's head, ruffling its woolly fur. He clicked his tongue a couple of times, and the dog licked his hand as he had mine.

"Friendly little chap, isn't he?" he remarked, and when I didn't answer looked directly at me for the first time, his eyebrows raised. He looked almost friendly, or as close to it as he was likely to come, at least with me, and so I smiled and nodded.

"Yes, Sarge, he is." Horváth didn't seem to have realised how much the dog enjoyed having his chest rubbed, and it would hardly have been proper on my part to enlighten him. It's purest coincidence if I was jealous of the dog's affections.

"Hm," Horváth nodded. "Right, little fellow, back to your basket. Go on, lie down." The dog was well-trained; he trotted to his basket in the corner right away. I tried not to think about the methods Horváth might have employed to ensure his obedience.

Horváth beckoned me to the table. "Well?"

"Sarge?"

He nodded at the box. "Aren't you going to open it?"

Being Horváth, he said it as though I should have done the instant I'd entered the room, and what kind of idiot was I for not realising? "Yes, Sarge."

I opened the box. Blue-black steel and golden brass gleamed inside.

"Well?" said Horváth. "What's that?"

"A gun, Sarge."

"What *kind* of gun, Countess?"

"A Roth-Steyr pistol."

"No." He wagged a finger. "Incorrect. That is not a Roth-Steyr pistol, Countess. It's a collection of parts and bullets. Yes?"

"Yes, Sarge."

"Then you know what to do, don't you?"

"Assemble it?"

Horváth clapped. "Bravo. On with it, then, your ladyship." He took a stopwatch out of his pocket and set it running. "You have one minute."

So this was it? Just another of his endless tests and exercises? Compared to some of the ones he'd put us through, this was nothing. I'd both dismantled and reassembled Roth-Steyrs – perhaps even this very one – on several occasions with less time to spare and under far worse conditions.

I fitted the pieces together, then pulled back the bolt, fitted bullets into a stripper clip and pushed them down into the gun, as I've just done in the toilet at the coffee shop – a few seconds ago, and a hundred years later. I slid the bolt forward, and the Roth-Steyr was loaded.

Horváth chuckled and applauded softly. "Congratulations, Countess. That's it. You're all done. Finished."

"Finished?" Had I made some last-second error and disqualified myself from the squad?

"Completed," he said. "Your training's done. You've passed." He motioned to the pistol. "You'll walk the Sindelar Gate tomorrow."

"Tomorrow?" I felt dizzy: over the past weeks this monastic regime had become my life, the mission that lay beyond it fading to a sort of nebulous ideal. Now it was a reality. The true ordeal still lay ahead.

"Tomorrow," said Horváth. "You've proven yourself. You're *Falkenjaeger* now."

That second was one of the happiest I've ever known. I might not have *wanted* to desire Horváth's approval, but I did. I knew a whole second, maybe two, of unadulterated triumph and joy; so much so that I very nearly didn't hear what he said next.

"Almost."

Imagine you're in flight, free and airborne; then suddenly your wings are gone and you fall to earth.

The angels sing, and then they weep. That was how I felt.

Horváth stepped sideways; the dog looked up at me from licking himself and wagged his tail. Horváth looked back to me, then motioned to the pistol.

"Why?" I said.

Horváth sighed. "Because I've told you to. Because when you get them in your sights, when they know it's all up – oh, believe me, I know what'll happen. There'll be no dying with dignity for them – they'll pull out all the stops, wheel out all the sob stories, anything to make you hesitate. I need to know that when that happens, I can trust you to pull the trigger. And if you can't kill a fucking dog, how can I trust you to kill a man?"

"A dog's innocent."

"Then I'll know you can kill the guilty, Countess. If you can't do that, I might as well shoot you now myself, because they won't hesitate. So?"

Yes, I could have walked out – and what then? Sever myself forever from Ulrich, from Tibor? And yes, my pride was at stake, too, after having striven so long and hard, as a woman, to prove myself. But on the other pan of the scale was the little dog, with his woolly coat and melting eyes.

There was a click and the stopwatch began ticking. "You've one minute, Countess. After that, you're out."

I already knew there was only one decision I could make. Not only because anything else would have been a betrayal of my training, the squad, even the Emperor, but because the Sindelar Gate's very existence was only known to a select few who could be trusted, and lacking the necessary resolve to complete the mission would almost certainly remove me from that category. If I failed this final test, I doubted I'd ever leave Aehrenbach; the grounds were extensive, with plenty of room for an unmarked grave.

I picked up the Roth-Steyr. Horváth raised an eyebrow. Behind him, the dog whined and cocked his head. Its head. I had to think of him as an it now; it was the only way I'd be able to do this. The dog whined again. I wanted to say something to him. It. Tell it something, before I did the deed. I couldn't, of course, not in front of Horváth. But nor could I look into those huge brown eyes.

And yet I had to look into them. If I didn't, how else could I aim? And besides, the least I could do was to acknowledge the price I was paying for what I wanted, whether or not I wanted it still. I owed him that much. It. Him. It.

Him.

The dog's eyes were huge and dark. He whined again. It whined again. It cocked its head to one side. He cocked his head to one side.

*I'm sorry*, I thought, wishing he could hear, then raised the gun.

A gentle squeeze, and the trigger gave way beneath the pressure from my finger. It gave and just for the tiniest instant nothing happened; the infinitesimal measure of time between the striker being released, and it hitting the primer on the cartridge. The firing pin on the tip of the striker would pierce the primer. The primer would explode, and the bright hot sparks from that explosion would be directed into the cartridge, where they would ignite the propellant charge inside. That in turn would trigger a second, more powerful explosion, the force of which would pop the copper-jacketed lead bullet from the neck of the cartridge, like a champagne cork from the neck of its bottle. The rifling grooves inside the barrel would cause the bullet to spin and thereby maintain a straighter and more accurate path in flight, until it left the muzzle at a speed of eleven hundred feet per second, faster than sound.

I remember the gunshot, huge and loud in that narrow space. The sound of it should have deafened me, but I still heard the sound of the bullet hitting flesh and bone, like the noise of a woodman's axe biting into a tree-trunk. I heard, too, the dog yelp once as the impact flung him backwards, and the ugly thump of his small body again the far wall like a limp doll of woolly grey rag – woolly grey rag now turning red – before it tumbled bonelessly to the floor.

And all the while, all the while, I kept my face like stone, knowing that Horváth watched with greedy, avid eyes, hungry for any sign of weakness he could use to deny me what he'd promised only a minute before.

At least the dog was dead, as quickly and as free from pain as I'd been able manage; I'd been able to give my newly and briefly found friend that much. Or so I thought, until he began to howl.

It didn't sound human in the least, but it *felt* human, if that makes any sense. A terrible high-pitched howl became an agonised whimpering. The worst thing about it wasn't the dog's pain, but his confusion. He didn't understand why; I could almost believe he was asking – more in sorrow than in anger, as the saying goes – for an explanation. He kicked and thrashed about as though the pain was a trap he was trying to escape.

From the corner of my eye I saw Horváth watching, an eyebrow raised as though to ask *Well? Are you going to leave the job half-finished, Countess? Typical aristo, expecting the* hoi polloi *to do whatever you can't be bothered to. Well, no: this you'll have to take care of yourself, if you want to walk the Gate.*

The dog, in all his writhing agony, was looking up at me. Pleading, or so I thought: it was hard to read those big, supplicating eyes as doing anything else. For what? It could have been for me to stop, or to help him, or to tell him why. It might even have been for me to forgive him whatever he'd done wrong to deserve this, because dogs are so trusting. Or it might have simply been for me to end it.

In the end, I chose – choose – to believe it was the last.

I aimed again, and fired again. There was another high-pitched, squealing yelp. I fired a third time, and continued to fire until the Roth-Steyr's magazine was empty. The dog had fallen silent long before then, but I continued to pull the trigger. I couldn't seem to stop. I wanted to make sure and besides, I was picturing Horváth's face in the dog's stead because it was the only way I could do it.

When the smoke cleared, the torn, bloody remains, half-huddled on the floor and half-splattered up the wall, innards steaming in the cold damp air, were almost unrecognisable. But not completely. I am not quite sure if, all these years later, the emotions provoked by that sight have ever quite left me, or if I will ever be able to say that I am no longer marked by it.

I released the bolt on the Roth-Steyr and let it snap forward, then made to set the weapon back down on the table. "No," said Horváth.

I looked up at him. "That's yours now," he said. "You've earned it." For once there was no sarcasm in his tone or his expression, no mockery. There might even have been a kind of sadness, a sort of pity. Was that respect in his eyes, the respect I'd craved for so long while at the same time hating him? In retrospect, it's hard to tell. I was numb and nauseated, filled with hatred and a horrible kind of triumph, all at once. And at the same time I had to maintain an icy, impassive mien, so that Horváth would see what I thought he wanted to see – someone who could master – or should that be mistress? – herself, whose will and duty and devotion to the Emperor was all.

He produced a holster for the pistol, on a leather belt. I put it on, and holstered the gun. There were webbing pouches for ammunition and clips. I loaded the stripper clips without needing to be told, stowed them in the pouches and straightened up before the sergeant.

"Tomorrow you walk the Gate," he said. "Well done, Countess. Dismissed."

And he saluted me. He had never done that before. I returned his salute, turned smartly and marched out.

I wonder, sometimes, if that final little act of cruelty was for himself as much as us, to sever himself from us as it severed us from him.

I marched past my fellow recruits, who all stared at me. They would have heard the gunshots, but nothing else. I nodded to Ulrich and Tibor, but that was all I could manage. I had to maintain my demeanour for a little longer.

I maintained it, in the event, until I reached the nearest lavatory. And there I vomited, retching and retching until only yellow bile, then air, came up. Kneeling before the white throne as if praying for forgiveness. And then I cried for what I'd done, muffling my face in my pillow to ensure the sound wouldn't carry beyond the door.

I still see that little dog's face sometimes. His face is with me now with particular vividness, though, a vividness I haven't experienced in decades, as I sit in the coffee-shop toilet with the pistol that killed him cradled in my hands. The metal gleams, shiny and blue-grey. The wooden grips show a few signs of wear, but that's all.

It's aged almost as well as me.

So now I'm armed. Now I've taken up the gun again. Now another part of my past has woken, and continues to exert its influence over me.

I thought, that day, that I was showing courage and resolution. Perhaps the real courage, the real resolution, would have been to throw down the gun at Horváth's feet and walk out with my head held high.

I'd be long dead, and so would the dog. One of the others in the squad would have killed him and even if they hadn't, how many years more would he have lived? But none of that matters. It was my choice that counted that day.

Of course, if I despise that choice and its results so much, there's an easy solution. Only one thing can kill me, and I'm holding it. I could do it now – put the barrel in my mouth and… bang. But no. I could do it, I can picture it even, but I don't want to. I do, it seems, still want to live. I want to continue my work, or penance, whatever it is, and I want to be with you for as long as cruel Time permits it.

And to do that, it seems, I will need this gun.

———

You'll be at work by now, so I go home. I'd like to keep the gun with me, but it's too risky to take it to the hospital. For now, the safest bet seems to be hiding it in our house. Another secret, and an intrusion, this ugly instrument of death lying in our home.

You hate guns. We both saw our share of gunshot wounds of a Saturday night in our time, and you lost a cousin to violence when you were in your teens. Wrong place, wrong time, carrying a bag of weed in his backpack as he biked down the street for fifty quid. Someone wanted to send a message to the man who'd paid him, so out they stepped and bang bang bang went their gun. The work of seconds, and a life snuffed out. Cut short. Futures eradicated – the loves he might have shared, the children he might have fathered, the good he might have done. So simple, the squeeze of a trigger. So complex and far-reaching, the impact of the deed.

But we need the gun, to be safe. That isn't paranoia, it's a fact. I still have time before my shift starts, so home I come.

I let myself in and draw breath in the empty house. Where to hide it? It has to be somewhere you won't find it, but somewhere where I can get to it quickly if I must.

The fireplace, I realise. There's no fire there any longer; instead there's a vase filled with honesty and other dried flowers. I fetch the toolbox from under the kitchen sink, move the vase aside, and lie on my back, my head in the fireplace, a small torch held between my teeth. I take the tack hammer and three nails and pound them into the brickwork. Old soot hisses and splatters down, dislodged by the impact. It might have been up there, I muse, since before I walked the Gate.

The bullets and spare clips are in a drawstring bag I found; I hang them from one of the nails. Then I unwrap the Roth-Steyr from its cloth and hang that there too: one nail fits through the trigger-guard, while the barrel rests on another one and the butt against the third, keeping it in place.

"Val?" you call, and I go still.

I can hear the thump of your footsteps on the landing. I look up the chimney again. The Roth-Steyr is anchored firmly. Is it firm enough? I reach out and prod it. It wobbles slightly, but holds. Have I loosened it now? Will it fall out when we're sitting there quietly one evening?

"Val?" you call again, and the stairs begin to creak. "Who's there?" you call, and I can hear the nervousness in your voice.

Have I time to escape? I could rush back into the kitchen with the toolbox and groundsheet, let myself out the back. Change out of the boiler-suit at work. That would be possible. But the latest creak I hear comes from halfway down the stairs: I know the house as I know your body, which is to say intimately and in detail, and I don't think I'll make it. I might, but I can't be sure, and if you catch me it'll look far more guilty than if you find me now. I can talk my way out of this. Tell you some story. What's one more lie, after all?

I keep my iPod in my jeans pocket – I have enough time, at least, to shove the earbuds in place and cue up some heavy metal before sticking my head back in the grate. Almost enough, anyway: as I move I see the door open and glimpse your arm. Did I glimpse your face? More to the point, did you glimpse me? What have you seen and what do you know now?

I hear you call my name over the music in my ears, but only just. I only react when you crouch down and put your hand on my knee, and I make sure I do so as violently as possible.

"Fuck!" I yelp and jackknife into a sitting position, or at least try to, cracking my head on the fireplace. You give a little yelp of distress, startled either by my reaction or the injury. "Jesus," I say, struggling free of the fireplace and clutching my forehead. "What the fuck are you doing here?"

"Oh, thanks, darling. What the fuck are *you* doing here?"

My lie's a good one because it's nearly the truth. "I got my hours mixed up," I say. "I don't actually start till eleven today. So I came back. Thought I heard something up there. Like a bird or something."

"A bird? What, you mean like trapped up there?"

"Thought it sounded like it."

You eye the hammer in my hand, an eyebrow raised. "And what were you planning to do with that, put it out of its misery?"

"Nah." I get up. "There's no bird. Some of the crap in there just worked itself loose."

You look at me, frowning, knowing something isn't right but unable to pinpoint what. That's when I finally notice how you look: pasty and dull-eyed and queasy. The perfect excuse to change the subject. "Anyway, sod that," I say, feeling disgusted with myself even though my concern's genuine, because I'm exploiting it. "What about you? How come you're home alone? You not well?" I can tell you're not, but I put my hand to your forehead. It's clammy and cold.

"Something I ate," you say. "I was halfway to work when it kicked in. Had to turn back." You offer a weak, sickly smile. "Needed a change of clothes. Don't worry, they're already in the wash."

"Oh, sweetheart." I hug you tightly, feeling you limp and hot in my embrace; I wish I could fix this, hate to see you suffer, but at the same time thank God you're ill and feel like crap because otherwise I'd never get this past you. "You called in sick?"

"Course I have. Cancelled all me clients for today. Probably norovirus. Not gonna be grateful if they end up shitting through the eye of a needle." You hold me at arm's length and look at me. "Oh God, you're gonna get it too."

"Might not," I tell you. "I feel okay." I won't get sick, of course, I never do. I can't, not since the Gate. There are actually times I miss it, believe it or not. The ordinary debilitation of the common cold, or influenza – not the kind that came after the war's end, though. God, that one was monstrous. But I miss being tucked up in bed and fussed over with tea and hot soup, with no expectation to do anything other than to take it easy.

"Maybe you should call in sick," you say. "Be on the safe side."

I want to; God, I want to. But what if there's a new break in the case? Another body wheeled in? But how can I say no to you?

I'm still trying to find a way when I realise that, on the other hand, I might be better off staying home. After all, if someone wants to come for me, where better than at home where I know the territory perfectly? The lie of the land, the entrances and the exits. No, I can't get sick, but you don't need to know that and nor does anyone else. the symptoms will be easy enough to counterfeit.

And this way, too, I'll be able to keep you safe.

"Okay," I say. "Give me a sec."

I ring the lab and give Dr Sharma the sob story. "Oh, you poor thing," she says. "Look after yourself. Remember, plenty of fluids. Replace your electrolytes."

"Aye, aye, Cap'n," I tell her, reminding myself I need to sound all weak and woozy.

"I'll give Mr Veale a kiss from you."

"Ugh. Christ," I say, "we've not got more dead bodies, have we?"

"We're a mortuary, Val. That's kind of the whole point of us."

"No, I meant anyone else shot with some sort of weird old bullet. We seemed to be full of them."

"We had two. Exactly two. And no, there haven't been any more."

"Thank fuck for that."

"Anyway, never mind that, Val. Rest up and get better. Give my love to Louise."

"Will do."

Perhaps I will counterfeit the symptoms, if I can – ideally as you're recovering. Then I can be fussed over. But the business with the fireplace is forgotten, at least.

Lying in bed with you later that same night, I'm unable to sleep. You've managed to, finally – or rather sheer exhaustion's finally caught up and had its wicked way with you. It's a relief to see that sweet little face in repose again. Relaxed, and not drained and strained and suffering. You look so vulnerable and young, almost like a child. At that moment, I love you perhaps more than I ever have. After all, you're a child to me in some ways – I know the ways and wickednesses of this world better than you can or are ever likely to. And God, I wish I could tell you the truth.

But it's the old mantra: I can't, and even if I could, you'd never believe me, and even if you did where would I even begin?

Well, that question, at least, I can answer.

I'd begin with Mayerling.

———

Mayerling was the official hunting lodge of the Imperial and Royal family of Austria-Hungary, and it was there that the Crown Prince Rudolf, heir to the Dual Monarchy's throne, had gone to stay, joining his friend Count Hoyos for a few days of hunting and shooting.

There was, however, another and unannounced guest: Baroness Mary Vetsera, the seventeen year old daughter of the Baron Albin Vetsera. The Crown Prince was nearly twice her age, and already married to the Princess Stephanie of Belgium, albeit far from happily. To make matters worse, he had – like his father and so many other Viennese men – conducted a series of affairs, though often with far less discretion than old Franz-Joseph – and dallied with prostitutes. Not only had he managed to contract venereal disease as a result – no joke in those pre-antibiotic days – but he'd passed it on to his wife, which among other things rendered her sterile. That wasn't good news for the dynastic succession of the Habsburgs, as Rudolf and Stephanie had only produced one child, the Archduchess Elisabeth, and only a man could inherit the throne – stupid rule if you ask me, but no-one did.

But that was all academic: Rudolf would never be Emperor, and the dynasty was doomed to fall. On the morning of January 30th, 1889, the bodies of the Crown Prince and the Baroness were found in the Prince's chambers. Both had died of gunshot wounds to the head, shattering their skulls.

A suicide pact, or so it seemed – not that that's stopped the conspiracy theories flying thick and fast over the years that have followed. But it's the simplest explanation. Rudolf was a troubled man, depressed and melancholic – a highly sensitive individual completely unsuited for the life he'd been born for. Mary Vetsera was only one of his mistresses, but unlike most of them she honestly thought she was different, she was special, she was the one. Most of all, she believed that she was the one he was going to leave his wife for. The old jokes are the best, aren't they?

Rudolf's affairs had never been conducted discreetly – Stephanie had been publicly humiliated by his actions more than once – but Mary was blatant in a way the others weren't. That mostly came from her; she was a seventeen-year-old girl, in some ways old beyond her years and in others fatally naïve, having spent most of her life being used as a social bargaining chip by her mother. The Vetseras, you see, were part of the 'second society.'

God, how should I explain all this to you, my lovely Louise, if I was to tell you the truth? People say the British are class-conscious, but they had nothing on the Hapsburg Monarchy. The 'second society' were what you might call *nouveau riche* – recently ennobled families, who, titles or no, didn't have the social standing or cachet of older families like mine, who had been oppressing the masses since the early Middle Ages. *We* got to mingle with the inner circles of Viennese society, and got comparatively easy access to the Imperial Family itself. Baroness Hélène Vetsera wanted that for her family, and her daughters – Mary especially – were a means to an end.

But Mary was still a teenage girl, and like so many of them she was impressionable, headstrong and romantic, devouring French novels of doomed and passionate love left and right. If she'd been around today the poor cow would be reading *Twilight*. Sometimes death's a mercy. So, big surprise – when she got together with Rudolf she built it all up in terms of the highest romance. He, trapped in a loveless marriage; she, a pawn in her mother's social-climbing games – they were meant to be together.

Quite how Mary thought Rudolf was going to divorce the wife who'd borne his child and remarry to make her, Mary, a future Empress of the devoutly Catholic Austrian Empire – the Emperor's title was, after all, 'His Imperial and Royal *Apostolic* Majesty' – I have no idea. But then again, at that age, you're prone to magical thinking. And you really believe that love will conquer all. I know I felt that way about Katrin. At the age of fourteen, I was utterly resolved that she and I were to spend our lives together. The class distinction, together with the problem of our both being women, were minor inconveniences to be overcome with a little fortitude and determination. I was disillusioned soon enough – Katrin married one of the footmen and pupped a litter of wailing brats and it couldn't have ended any other way, really – but for a few months, a little golden spell, I was blissfully happy and thought my future already certain and secured. The shape my life would in fact take could never have occurred to me.

Oh, for God's sake, listen to me rabbit on. None of this has the slightest relevance, except to illustrate that

Mary Vetsera was the closest thing to an innocent in the game.

There were stories about Rudolf, that he'd been involved in some sort of plot with Hungarian secessionists. He was a melancholy sod anyway, drinking heavily and drugging himself half to oblivion. He'd asked another of his mistresses to die with him – Mitzi Caspar, who'd been with him long before (and during) his dalliance with Mary. Poor kid, it was never what she thought it was.

Anyway, when the bodies were found it was a scandal of the first magnitude, despite all attempts to cover it up. They gave out that the Crown Prince had died alone from heart failure, bundling Mary's naked body into a spare room. Her family smuggled her out of Mayerling in a carriage, propped upright between two of her uncles, and she was buried in secret.

Some said she'd killed him, then herself; others that it had been an assassination. But the facts pointed to Rudolf having killed Mary and then taken his own life. Even then there were stories – of a debauched party where she bridled at his putting her on show, only to be shot for her pains – but it was largely presumed to be a suicide pact. The Habsburgs tried to hush the whole business up and only made it worse.

As I said before, I even have the Mayerling incident to thank for my name. The affair between Rudolf and Mary was facilitated by Countess Marie Larisch von Moennich, who was close friends with Mary and an illegitimate niece and confidante of Rudolf's mother, the Empress Elisabeth. She usually needed more money than her husband gave her, so Rudolf paid her bills and in return she acted as the lovers' go-between; when that came out after the suicide, the Emperor and Empress would have nothing more to do with her, and the nobility in general followed their lead. Ostracised, she moved to Bavaria, then America, then back again, dying in poverty in a German nursing home.

My mother was one of her few former friends – one of the few members of Austrian society as a whole – who'd give Marie Larisch the time of day after Mayerling, albeit only on what would today be called 'the down-low'. I believe Mama felt Larisch had been ill-served, and helped her when and how she could.

When I was born, in May 1889, Mama named me after Larisch's eldest daughter, Marie Valerie. Calling me Marie would have been a step too far, as it had been not only Larisch's first name but the late Baroness Vetsera's, but it was a small, subtle 'fuck you' gesture to the powers that be, probably the most outrageous act of rebellion Mama ever performed in her life. Not that the Emperor and Empress – or anyone else that I knew of – ever noticed. Even so, Mama told me – one evening, after several glasses of good Tokay – it made her feel better.

Anyway, that's the story of my name.

There've been conspiracy theories and wild stories galore about Mayerling, although a few years ago Mary's letters came to light, confirming that it had been a straightforward suicide pact between her and the Crown Prince. Rudolf wanted to die; he just hadn't wanted to do so alone. Romantic double suicides were the in-thing at the time; ever heard of Elvira Madigan? There's a Mozart symphony named after her, which isn't a bad feat considering he died long before she was born.

Except…

(Drum roll)

There's more to it than that.

Don't get me wrong – well, you know me as well as anyone, lies notwithstanding, and you know I subscribe to the cock-up as opposed to the conspiracy theory of history. But now and again there is a conspiracy, and it's real. To be fair, there wasn't a shortage of them in Central Europe in the run-up to World War One.

A group of young Army officers, who called themselves – try not to laugh – the Black Eagles of the Crownlands, decided that Things Had Gone Quite Far Enough, Thank You. Decadence and softness, liberalism and democracy, were destroying the Empire from within. They still regarded Rudolf as the hope of the future (they weren't close enough to the heart of things to know that Princess Stephanie was now infertile or just how much of a disease- and drug-ridden wreck the Crown Prince had become), but thought he had been led astray by malign influences – foreign agents, decadent modernists, liberals, freethinkers and Jews. Like I said before, the old jokes are the best.

Young people can be very naive and simplistic in their ideas, and the Black Eagles of the Crownlands were no exception, but on the other hand I wasn't much better at that age. Their Grand Plan To Arrest The Moral Decline Of The Habsburg Empire essentially boiled down to 'kill everyone who's leading the Crown Prince astray'.

Young folks like that, so eager to kill or die for this or that golden calf: small wonder the Great War fed and ravened for so long. Gavrilo Princip, the man who shot the Archduke and started that whole horrendous carnival of death, was only nineteen. Practically a fucking child. If Franz Ferdinand had gone to Sarajevo a month later Princip would have been shot, but he became a murderer twenty-seven days short of his birthday, and under Habsburg law, the death penalty could only be imposed on those aged twenty or over.

So instead they imprisoned him at Terezin, where he developed skeletal tuberculosis: they had to amputate his right arm and he only weighed forty kilograms when he finally gave up the ghost, aged twenty-three, seven months before the war's end. Poor stupid little bastard.

But then, were the older generation any better? No. Wide-eyed *naïfs* with guns on the one hand, and cruel, cynical old men on the other...

The name at the top of the Black Eagles's death-list was Mary Vetsera – or, as one surviving communication referred to her, 'that parvenu Greek slut': flaunting her affair with Rudolf so publicly, she embodied, to them, all that was wrong. Blaming the woman: never goes out of fashion, does it? So they slipped into Mayerling and entered Rudolf's chambers when he wasn't there. Two of them pinned Mary to the bed and the third shot her in the temple. A neat little wound going in, and a massive one going out.

Then they slipped out again, leaving Rudolf to find the body. I have no idea what reaction they expected him to have – I heard stories, during our training for the Gate, that they'd left a note exhorting Rudolf to mend his ways and be the heir they all wanted him to be, but we were never clear whether or not that was just a rumour. Either way, the effect of the assassination wasn't what they'd hoped. Rudolf sat with Mary's body for several hours, then took his revolver and shot himself.

The Black Eagles disbanded after that – their *raison d'etre* was fucked for a start, and besides they did *not* want, under any circumstances, to be traced. They did – at the time – a decent job of covering their tracks. And besides, the authorities were more concerned with preventing a scandal than carrying out a proper forensic investigation.

The suicide story was the one they went with, the attempts to conceal Mary's presence having dismally failed. It was considered less appalling than to reveal that the Emperor's own soldiers could have been responsible. Mary Vetsera's family certainly believed it had been a suicide pact; I'm not even sure if the Emperor and Empress ever learned the truth. The Empire would cling to life for a few decades more, but Mayerling was one of the wounds that would ultimately bleed it white, and one of the tumbling dominoes that would eventually begin the First World War. Rudolf had been liberal and pro-Hungarian; with him gone and Franz Ferdinand (who was neither of those things) now lined up for the succession, the tensions only grew worse.

The old Emperor, Franz Joseph, was one of the longest-reigning monarchs of all time, spending nearly sixty-eight years on the throne all told. But in 1916, at the age of eighty-six, he caught a cold after a walk in the park at Schönbrunn, and it turned into pneumonia. He died from it, and that was the end of an era.

His nephew, Karl, succeeded to the throne, reigning for just under two years. He did what he could to end the war and keep the Empire together, but it was a lost cause. Towards the end of his reign, he learned – I don't know how – the truth about Mayerling.

Emperor Karl wasn't a vengeful man. He genuinely sought peace, but without success, and in his short reign saw the Empire entrusted to him crumbling. He'd been placed in a role he was unequal to, and in which he could only fail.

He did his best, however, poor though that was, and he won one war, secret and unknown to all but a few. And that victory saved countless lives.

Some of the Black Eagles still lived, many of them in influential military and civil service roles, and a handful of them still kept some version of their old faith. By 1917, the Eagles had reformed[1], recruiting a new cadre of young officers to act as their footsoldiers in a new assassination programme. The target, this time, was the Emperor himself. Another Habsburg could easily be found: it was the Empire that must continue.

But Austria's Great Power days were done; the only question now was how long it had left, and how painful the end would be. As it was, revolutions, counter-revolutions, border conflicts and civil wars would plague Central Europe for half a decade after the Armistice was signed, but while the Black Eagles could never have succeeded, the price that would have been paid for their attempt would have been horrific beyond calculation.

Luckily, the Imperial and Royal Intelligence Service, the *Evidenzbureau*, remained loyal to Karl. On learning of the conspiracy, the last Habsburg Emperor acted quickly and decisively for once in his reign, and declared war on the Black Eagles of the Crownlands.

---

1   No, not the band. They haven't been around *that* long. V von B-V.

Arrests, secret trials, summary executions – and in a few cases, outright assassination – followed, and by 1918, the last of the Black Eagles's original founders was dead. Most of their young men, too. But not all.

Twenty or thirty of them were still unaccounted for by the final year of the war, following a brief, disastrous guerilla campaign. By then, even they could see nothing could arrest the Empire's disintegration, but they saw its collapse as the end of a battle, not a war. A new dawn would come, one in which the Monarchy's time would come again. They would see to it.

Yep, you're probably thinking what I'm thinking – what drugs were these people on? But now I wonder. Things do go in cycles, after all: freedom and democracy seem to be passing out of vogue, and in their place come brave new worlds or brave old ones, the familiar authoritarian wet dreams of empire…

I don't know, exactly, when or how the Sindelar Gate was discovered, or how the Black Eagles made it theirs. But they did, and they used it.

As far as the devoutly Catholic Karl was concerned, the Gate could only be a form of black magic, meaning the Black Eagles had added blasphemy to their crimes. But using it, they could wait for decades, even centuries, until their enemies were dust, before trying to rebuild the Empire once more. And while Karl wanted to preserve that Empire, he wouldn't do so through them.

The Sindelar Gate, together with its creator and his assistants (of whom more later), was captured. Karl finally agreed to make use of it with great reluctance and after having obtained the blessing of the Catholic Church (I have no idea how.)

I was working for the *Evidenzbureau* at the time. After Franz and Conrad died, I wanted to do something, and I was pretty ashamed of the frivolous, hedonistic lifestyle I'd led (that wore off, as you've probably guessed.) I'd helped locate and dispose of several Black Eagles. I first heard of the *Falkenjaeger* when Tibor told me that he and Ulrich had been recruited, at which point I went directly to Colonel Ronge – the head of the *Evidenzbureau* – and asked to join them too. The other recruits were all men, but the Colonel took the view a female agent would be useful. So, that was how my involvement began.

And it lasted from the end of the First World War to the end of the Second.

———

A fortnight after I parted company from the others for the last time, I was crossing the Swiss border – the same day your mother was born, if I'm remembering her birthday correctly – having raided a cache of diamonds and rubies in order to grease palms and pay for life's various necessities. Ulrich, Tibor and Erick could have the other caches; let them carry on, if they so wished. Besides, I was pressed for time.

What would Horváth have said if he could have seen me? Probably snorted that he'd been right all along, that this was what happened when you sent a woman to do a man's job. Or maybe he would have been disappointed, even saddened; in his twisted way, I think he'd come to have some form of respect for me, even affection. I preferred to imagine my actions sending him into a potentially-fatal apoplexy.

In Switzerland, I banked and invested my funds, and had papers made up under several different identities. I wasn't sure what I would do next, but it seemed only sensible to lay the groundwork for it.

It wasn't enough, I concluded, to withdraw from the games of death: there had to be reparation of some kind. I'd spent years in Death's service; now it was time to fight for the other side.

There were still refugees and displaced persons all across Europe, so I worked in some of the camps and relief agencies for them. I left Europe for a while in the late 1940s for the Middle East, to assist UNRWA in the Palestinian refugee camps, then made my way back to Europe. I couldn't face Vienna or Budapest – too many memories, and what if Ulrich or Tibor or the others were there? So I travelled northward for a spell – Denmark, Finland, Sweden, Norway – before making my way through Belgium, Holland, France.

I spread this over years, you understand. Decades. By the mid 1970s it was time to move on from France, and I had to choose my next home. Somewhere I'd never been before, I decided; somewhere new.

Spain and Portugal I'd already spent time in – they'd been neutral lands during the War, therefore a useful place to hide – and while Russia, China and Mongolia were all technically possible, I wasn't sure I wanted to risk exposing my fake identities to the scrutiny of a totalitarian state.

The USA was a temptation, and Canada, and the warmer lands of Central and Latin America. There was Australia, too, and I'd never visited Africa. But in the end, it was Britain that called.

Britain, that other Empire, the only one whose territories I'd never set foot in till then. And I fell in love, I'll admit it. God knows why, but then love is hardly a rational phenomenon, is it? Could either of us break down, on a form or a test, what it is about one another that makes us crazy? I know I couldn't – but who really knows what goes on in someone else's head? It's not as if you know half of what's in mine. My true past – at once utterly irrelevant to who we are together, but fundamental too, the wedge driving between us…

Well, no. The real wedge there is time, isn't it? It forces my lovers along its stream like twigs while I stay fixed like a rock, only able to watch them borne away out of sight. Unless I chose a fellow immortal, of course – but even leaving aside the fact that cock is something of a deal-breaker for me, Tibor was gay and the rest? Ugh, no, thank you.

But, in any case – Britannia. I look at it now, after forty years plugged into this particular socket, and the parallels are there, all too clear to see. The sinking back into a black, poisonous nostalgia for Golden Ages of purity and grandeur that never were. The self-inflicted wounds, born out of the nation's own internal contradictions, while on the grander stage old alliances falter and old orders pass. Nothing new under the sun, just endless revolutions of the same old wheel.

I thought the time of the great empires had passed, that democracy was to be the new way. I certainly hoped, after the fascist pipedreams had fallen in rubble and blood, that this would be the case, and yet all those hopes and values have been steadily pissed away. Maybe they were only ever dreams too, and 'might makes right' is the only truth.

Then again, nationalism was the other thing that helped break the Habsburg Empire, and that hasn't gone away – on the contrary, it festers Europe-wide and across the Atlantic too.

Yes. Sometimes, for all the technological advances and sexual liberation (another reason for Britain's appeal – under the staid and respectable veneer, you're some of the dirtiest people on Earth, and God knows I love you for it) it's far too like 1914 here, all over again…

But you do have your NHS, battered and belittled though it is. And that's where I've spent the past four – nearly five – decades, moving from city to city and name to name, changing hair and eye colour, ageing myself, then being born anew. I've brought children into the world, and helped the old and the dying take their leave of it with kindness and care. I've helped men and women with terrible injuries recover, and I've helped those for whose afflictions there's been no cure die in peace and dignity. I've changed the tattered Imperial standard for that of the little people, the ordinary ones. I've stood on picket lines, marched against wars, and been proud to do so. And I've found you. All from breaking my dead oath and going my own way.

Thirty years serving death and seventy serving life: does that balance the scales, maybe even tip them in my favour? It's become a habit, anyway. Maybe transferring to Pathology was the sin that brought the past to my door – not adding to the ranks of the dead, but no longer giving succour to the living. Because look what's been wheeled in front of me lately, and look where I am…

I go back to work at the end of the week. I'm perfectly well, after all, and I chafe without work to occupy me – the house is scrubbed clean and gleaming, everything tidied away and in a place – but that isn't the real reason.

I think you know something. Am I wrong? Is there any way I can find out without ruining everything? I don't know what it is you know or think you know, but I think you've guessed I've lied about something, that some part of my carefully-constructed lie has begun to unravel. And so I want to go back to work because then that'll be less time we spend together, less opportunity for you to catch me out or see something else to feed your suspicions.

And yes, there's the whole Roth-Steyr business. First Erick, then Tibor. Who else? I've made the odd call to Dr Sharma, ostensibly just checking all is well, but by the third or fourth time she was exasperated. "For God's sake, Val – honestly, we can handle it. The department won't fall apart without you. Just stay home and get well."

Maybe Tibor was the last. Or maybe the hunt's moved on, and the killing's taking place elsewhere. But what if the storm changes course again, and comes back this way?

Whatever the case, I need to be back at work. There's still a sense of something in the air. Danger of some kind; menace. Just now I can't tell what. Is it from you, seeing past some of my deceptions? Is it from one band of immortals or another, fighting out the last of their war, with me in the middle trying to keep my head down and hoping I'm not noticed? I can't pin it down, but I've learned to trust this feeling when I get it.

Which causes a problem on my first day back. The worst of the diarrhoea and vomiting's stopped, but you're still pretty weak and woozy. Thing is, you still insist on coming downstairs – "I've been cooped up in bed all fucking week" – and sitting in your armchair in the front room, wrapped in your dressing gown, sipping tea and warily nibbling toast.

Which is awkward.

Because much as I love you and hate to be parted from you, I'm trying to make a decision here. No, correction to that – I've made my decision, but acting on it is a little difficult right now, what with you sitting in front of the fireplace and my needing to get the Roth-Steyr out of there.

It's bad enough having the thing in the house. Ever since I brought it back I've been on edge, but knowing the one object that could unravel everything we have is only kept from you by three nails in some century-old brickwork does not do wonders for a girl's peace of mind. Carrying the thing with me is worse still. So many ways it could be found, especially in these post-9/11, security-obsessed times. Even if you don't catch me with the gun, who else might? And then there's the fear – the fear, because I haven't fired the thing in years – that if I do draw the gun, some sudden sound will startle me and I'll fire in panic or without meaning to, and shoot the wrong person. An innocent. God forbid, a child. Or you. If I get up in the middle of the night, startled by a creaking floorboard, convinced someone's coming for me, and you come shuffling out in search of the toilet unannounced, the special ammunition in the Roth-Steyr will kill a mortal as efficiently as it will one of the deathless.

But there is danger. I know that there is danger. And it may take the form of whoever carries the other Roth-Steyr, and whomever that is, I'm going to need more than love and good wishes if I want to come home to you again. And I do. I very, very much do. So I kill time and wait to get you out of the room. I won't need long. A minute, no more. Not even that.

"You should get going," you say, tiredly. "You've been up all night, unable to sleep, even though you're exhausted from the last few days and nights. "You're gonna be late."

"I'll be okay," I tell you. "Advantage of an early shift. You miss the rush hour."

"Yeah, but it's not instant."

"I don't like leaving you, that's all." Which is true as well, and not even to do with whatever the threat is.

"Call in sick again, then."

"Nah. I do need to get back. I've been fine all week. I don't like taking the piss."

"I know you don't, love. So go on."

Is there something else in your voice, under the tiredness? A suspicion – or worse, a withdrawal? Have you already caught me in some lie and drawn conclusions from it, right or wrong? (Let's face it, the chances of your drawing the right ones, even in the near-psychedelic hallucinatory state of a fever, are pretty damned remote.) Is that the threat? If so, no gun will shield me.

I go to you and kiss your head, cradling you. You pat my hand. Is it just the weakness, the tiredness from being ill, or is it a perfunctory gesture, something done for form's sake, because you know I'm false? At times like this I feel wretched. I give you so little in return for so much. How can you *not* find me out?

And what does it say about me if you don't, other than how practised a liar I am?

Can I tell you? Can I share who I truly am? I'd have to figure out a demonstration, some way of convincing you that would be inarguable without being too traumatic? Oh God, I want you to know. I want there to be someone, outside this foetid little world of dead empires and megalomaniacal fantasy, to know me. Could it be you? Or is it too late?

"Go on," you say. "Get your arse out of here."

"Yeah, I will. In a sec. You sure there's nothing else I can get you?" No, Valerie, you cretin – I'm supposed to be getting you out of the room, not myself.

"I'm fine, hun."

"Okay," I say, thinking I'll have to go unarmed, maybe sneak back later on some pretext. But as I straighten up you put a hand to your stomach and struggle out of the chair. "Oh bloody hell," you mutter.

"Can I do—"

"I can go for a shit by myself, Val, honest. I was doing it for years before I met you."

You smile as you say it, so I'm more or less sure that's not some kind of barb.

"All right."

"I'll be fine. Now fuck off for God's sake, or you'll be late."

"Okay. Okay."

You're already out of the door – norovirus is an insistent master – and that's all I need. I kneel, slipping a hand up inside the chimney breast, and take down the gun. A hiss and rattle-patter of soot, my hand grimed and black, but I have the weapon and there's an old hand-towel tucked away in my shoulder-bag just for this purpose. I swaddle the Roth-Steyr in it, shove it in the bag and head out, calling a last goodbye as I go.

———

The mortuary's quiet. Dr Sharma's been called away to a staff meeting, but there's only one body, a patient from Geriatrics who died in the night. Not much for me to do, thank God.

I power up the computer and look over the notes on 'Unknown Males #236 and #247'. I find nothing I hadn't expected – two dead men, each shot twice in the head, no ID, no DNA match, no fingerprint match, no way of ever determining who they are. Were.

The one common factor: an 8mm Roth-Steyr, the twin of the one I've secured to my lower left leg with gaffer tape. I can feel the tape starting to loosen, but I think it'll hold a little longer, especially if I'm careful. Thank God Dr Sharma isn't here right now; I'm only absent for our occasional holidays, illness almost never being an issue, so I always feel awkward for the first couple of days back at work, even without a large and highly illegal firearm attached to my leg. I search for any other recent gunshot wound cases in the area, especially with unusual calibres, but find nothing. I briefly get my hopes up when I see one case involving a wound from a .32 automatic – 7.65mm if you're a European, a commonplace calibre but the same as the pistol that Ulrich always favoured. But it's just the usual all-too-human stupidity; some swaggering stupid lad with more testosterone than sense showing off and shooting his girlfriend through the hand. No fatal injuries there, thank God. But nothing to suggest that Janacek or Varga have met their end. Or Ulrich.

For which I suppose I should be thankful; however distanced we've become, he's my brother still, the last of the House of von Bradenstein-Vršovci.

Is it Varga or Janacek they were hunting – or could it really be both of them together? Could seventy-odd years have passed without one or the other of them being run to earth? But what does it matter? Dead is dead, and vengeance is sordid and ugly, a fool's game. But even so, especially when I think of my sweet, beloved Tibor, I am not immune to rage.

So nothing more is known. I shut off the computer. I was hoping some clue might have been found; if it's made Manchester too hot for the killer, he might have fled, which would at least have bought me some peace of mind. But there's no sign of that. Perhaps the hunt has moved on to other places. Perhaps I'll never know the end of it. I can live with that.

But I doubt somehow that that's the case.

I'm pulling a late shift tonight; it's a schoolnight towards the back end of the month, with payday a week away, so things are quiet: who has the money or the energy to get in trouble? So at least it's quiet. Dr Sharma's gone home, and good luck to her; as far as I know there are no dark, terrible secrets in her marriage, so may she have a pleasant evening of DVDs, Netflix, her takeaway of choice or a wild bondage session – whatever floats her boat, I do not judge. Somebody might as well have an uncomplicatedly good time, since I won't be.

I sit back with a good paperback and zone out, so much so that I barely hear the door open.

"Evening, Val."

"Inspector Reeve." I get up quickly. "You're up late."

"Yeah, sorry to disturb you." He yawns and rubs his eyes. "Burning the midnight oil a bit."

"The Roth-Steyr business?"

"How did you guess?" Is there a hint of suspicion there?

"Well, it's the only case that's brought you over here lately, unless there's been anything new in the last week. I've been off."

"I heard. You okay now?"

"Yeah. Norovirus. Lucky I was over it quickly."

"Your partner okay?"

What is this? Does he suspect something? I feel a cold, griping cramp in my innards: all of a sudden, the prospect of a very sudden end to this life, this identity, is before me. I should be able to get away easily enough – by brandishing the exact same make of rare firearm used in the murders at a police officer – but then I'll have to run. And it isn't fair to make a fugitive out of you too. "On the mend," I say. "She got it first, but worse than me. I've got a very good immune system."

"So I'm told, yeah. First sickness absence ever, Dr Sharma said. Literally."

"Yeah. I've been lucky. It was a nasty bug." What is this? Something isn't right. The Roth-Steyr shifts on my leg; I'm starting to sweat, and that's loosening the tape.

"Odd business, the whole thing," he says. "They keep me up at night, cases like this."

"Do they?"

"Mm." He looks at me. "I think we're quite alike in that."

"Are we? I just like to finish my shift and get home."

Reeve shakes his head. "No. I've seen you at work enough times. You're conscientious. Thorough. You like everything to make sense and be in a place."

"Who doesn't?"

"Some people like chaos. But it's a balancing act, isn't it? Can't be all of one or the other. Has to be a mix. Otherwise nothing changes. Nothing moves forward."

"No." I'm scared. I want to ask what he's doing here, but I'm afraid to hear the answer. That's stupid. What are the chances of Reeve working out the truth? Zero, unless he's gone mad. A madman can be dangerous, of course, but not to me. Not unless Reeve's got that other Roth-Steyr under his coat.

"Can't stop thinking about the murder weapon," he says. Fucking hell, is he reading my mind? "A Roth-Steyr pistol. I mean, they still turn up. Very well-made guns, and they made hundreds of thousands of them back in the day, but still. The ammunition's a bugger to get, and loading the thing? Forget it. You've got to shove a clip of bullets in through the chamber at the top. Not what your average gangster wannabe's going to be toting. Glocks are very in this year. This is strictly retro. This is like somebody's great-great granddad's World War One souvenir, or something. Like you'd get in a country house murder mystery."

"Only not in a country house," I say. I yawn, pretend to be tired, move out from behind the gurney that's between us. I'm not keen on removing the barrier between Reeve and me, but it gets me closer to the exit, and I've always preferred flight to fight.

"True," he says. "True." And he yawns too – it's a contagious thing, yawning, I yawn, you yawn, he yawns, everybody yawns – and he pushes his fingers through his hair.

Through his black, tangled hair.

Black and tangled.

It's the hair that does it. Ever since I met him there's been a nagging sense of familiarity about Detective Inspector Reeve, something I can't for the life of me place. An actor, a musician, a long-ago workmate, a politician? But it's none of those things.

Recognition is a funny thing. Put someone's face in a completely different context to the one you're used to seeing it in, and it can be impossible to place. Add enough weight – and he has to have gained two or three stone – and that robs the face of even more familiarity, softening the jawline and adding a chin, turning a once-lean physique to a thicker, stockier one.

And of course, he had a beard back then, a nice neat little beard which he's now shaved off. And I only ever saw his face in black and white official photographs, and once, at a distance, in Bucharest in 1929.

It's Varga.

Reeve is Varga.

"I have to go to the toilet," I say, and move past him quickly for the door. The back of my neck comes alive, waiting to feel a gun aimed at it, that or a move aimed at physical subjugation. I try to remember what Horváth taught us about hand-to-hand fighting. If the bastard makes a grab for me, can I knock him down? And then what? I can subdue him, knock him out, but what then?

He's not going to shoot me, I tell myself, not here in the middle of the hospital. He's not. He's not. Even if it's the middle of the night, and silent, and there's no-one around.

I push out through the doors and hear them flap shut behind me. Walk, Val, walk fast. Even if he has the gun, he's not going to shoot here. Unless he's got something to muffle the shot. And if you really thought there was no danger, why's your Roth-Steyr taped to your leg?

Down the corridor to the junction. Right for the toilet, left for the rest of the hospital. I glance back. Can't see Reeve – no, not Reeve, Varga – behind me, so I go left. Maybe that simple move will be enough.

Just up the way and to the left is the entrance to another department. I duck into the doorway, crouching, and start tugging at the pistol, wincing as the tape comes away from my leg, taking hair – maybe I should have shaved my legs after all – and threatening to take skin too. And as I do, I'm looking back the way I came.

I straighten up and hold my breath, press myself back and pray no-one else comes through, as Reeve, as Varga, emerges from the corridor I've just come from and glances left, then right. He doesn't see me. He doesn't see me. Then he turns right and goes towards the toilets.

His hand has slipped under his jacket.

Go left and I'm into the hospital. People, or as many people as I'll get here this late. In a crowd, I should be safe.

But it's over. My life with you. One way or the other. The brutal, immiserating awareness of that crashes in on me. If I get away, Varga comes after me. If I kill Varga – and he's killed Erick and Tibor, both of whom had had a sight more fresh experience than me – then I'm a killer and I'll have to run. Can't risk getting caught and locked away; what happens when I don't age? Immortal or not, I'm still only human: I've no particular powers for a prison breakout. No real powers at all, in fact, except that I don't age and can heal any wound.

All of sudden, I feel more vulnerable because of who I am, not less. Well , if I wasn't who I am I wouldn't have to worry about anything.

If I run, Varga will come after me, and then you'll be in danger too. I can't permit that.

I thought that by withdrawing from the game I was safe. It didn't occur to me that the Black Eagles, once hunted, might only feel safe with every hunter dead. Retired or not, I know their names and how to end them…

And besides, I have to know if Varga's alone. Is Janacek in the picture too? Should I be looking over my shoulder for him as well?

I can almost hear Horváth laughing as I crouch and finish pulling the Roth-Steyr from my leg. I ball up the tape and toss it aside. I should really take it to the incinerator.

With my free hand, I reach under my scrubs. Under them, I'm wearing my normal clothes. I shouldn't be, but there was always the chance I'd need to make a sudden getaway tonight. I take the little flip-phone from my jeans pocket, ring your number and start down the corridor after Varga.

"Valerie," you say. Immediately I go cold. Something's wrong.

"What's up, babe?"

"What did you hide up the chimney?"

Shit.

"It's a long story, love."

"I found a bullet, Valerie."

"What?" Shit. Shit shit shit. I stashed a few spare rounds of ammunition in a little niche I found in the chimney. Just in case. One must have fallen out. One is sometimes all it takes. One assassin with a pistol at Sarajevo. One survivor of the Sindelar Gate, from either side. One 8mm bullet.

"You've been acting off all month, and now this?"

"Louise—"

"You know how I feel about guns, Valerie." There's a cold finality in your voice, and it sets my stomach cramping up. This is it, then? The end? Convenient, perhaps, if I have to move on anyway, but I didn't want to end it like this. I wanted to find a way that we could part as friends, at least. Then your tone shifts. "What the fuck, Val? What the actual fuck?" Your voice is going ragged and I realise your control has broken: you're close to tears.

I hold the gun flat against my thigh, doing my best to hide it from any casual observers. I drop my voice down to a whisper as I move down the corridor, because I don't know where Reeve – where Varga – is right now and I can't afford to tip him off. I should end the call now and focus on him, but I know that everything I've had with you is hanging by a thread and I can't let that break, whatever the risk to myself. Horváth would either be killing himself laughing at this sight or shaking his head in despair. *Might as well put the gun to your temple and fire, Countess*, he'd say.

"It's a long story, darling," I say. "Very long." Longer than you can possibly know. But… but in the middle of all this my heart soars. Because I realise I have a chance here. I can simply tell the truth. You won't believe me, of course, but I can prove what I am. Wound myself with a knife, maybe, and show you it healing. There are ways and means. I doubt you'll still want me after that, be able to accept the truth or more accurately live with it, but we might part friends of some kind. And I'll have something I always wanted, however briefly: a lover who truly knows me, down to the bones.

"Val—"

"Listen to me, darling," I say. "Louise, I love you, okay? I fucking love you. But right now I cannot talk. Something very bad's happening. I'm gonna come home, when I've sorted this, and I'm gonna tell you everything. Everything. The whole truth, nothing but, all of that." Jesus Christ, stop fucking waffling, Val. "I'll tell you everything," I whisper again, "and then it's up to you. Whatever you want. But right now I have got to go."

"Val—"

"I love you," I say again, because if this goes sideways I want those to be the last words you hear me say. And then I break the connection and power down the phone and make my way down the corridor with a good two-handed grip on my Roth-Steyr.

---

All right. Now I need to focus. If I want to see you and tell you everything, I have to be alive to do it. Not on my back with holes in my head, like Erick and Tibor have been. Or as Ulrich might have. I push that thought aside. It's like meditation, in a way, only instead of an image of a sunny beach or a pool of clear water, I have to focus on Varga.

My plan, such as it is, is simple enough. Follow Varga's trail, while he thinks he's following me, get the drop on him – and then? I haven't killed in seventy-five years, but I'll have to. In the middle of a busy hospital, too, not a devastated city with bombs and bullets flying every which way. And then I'll get away and find you and tell you my story, and then I'll go.

I've reached the bend in the corridor that leads to the toilets. Breathing deeply, I peer round it. I can see nothing. I step out into the corridor, gun aimed ahead. Surely Varga must have reached the toilets by now and failed to find me. Surely he should be doubling back. Or maybe he hasn't gone in; maybe he's waiting outside.

As it turns out, it's neither. I don't know where he's hidden himself, but before I've gone another five paces down the corridor I hear a shoe scuff on the smooth floor and a small soft click that I know very well; it's the sound of the striker on a Roth-Steyr cocking, followed by Varga's soft voice saying "Please don't move."

I obey. For now. Not much else I can do but I'm going to have to do something else, and quickly, because otherwise – I think of Tibor, or Erick. But of Tibor most of all. I feel the gun's weight in my hand, trying to decide which way I should jump or drop or roll.

"I don't want to kill you, Countess," Varga says. "Please don't do anything silly. I'd prefer it if we could talk."

Wouldn't that be nice if it were only true? "Like you talked to Tibor? And Erick?" I add, and Erick's name is almost as an afterthought. I feel bad about that. But Tibor's death affects me the most.

"I didn't want to kill them either," he says. "I gave them the same choice I'm giving you now. Unfortunately, they wanted to kill me, and I don't want to die." He sighs. "Funny, isn't it, how persistent the urge to live is? I've considered suicide several times over the years, but I've never been able to go through with it."

That strikes a chord.

"Look," he says. "I'm serious. I don't want to kill you. I don't want to kill anyone any more. And no, I don't want to bring back the bloody Empire any longer either."

I half-turn my head at that and there's a short indrawn breath from Varga. "Christ, don't do that."

"Sorry," I say.

The strangest thing is that I believe him. Maybe it's because I want to, because I don't want to kill him either, partly because of all the mess and chaos it would involve, but partly because I just don't want to.

Did Tibor believe him? Or was it that Tibor couldn't afford to? Tibor was still hunting, after all; still at war. You can't believe a claim like that when you're still fighting.

But perhaps, perhaps I can.

"So what do we do?" I say.

"Turn around to face me, Countess. Very, very slowly."

Does he just not want to shoot me in the back? But we can all be slaves to hope, so I pivot slowly, keeping the pistol in the same position it's been in. As I turn, I realise I'll be pointing it at Varga's chest, and hesitate.

"It's all right," he says. "Keep going."

He has his gun in a two-handed grip, pointed at my head. My gun lines up with his chest. "So what now?" I say.

"Now," he says. "We lower our guns together."

He begins first, letting the pistol dip slowly groundwards. I follow suit, till both our weapons are pointing at the floor.

"And now?" I say.

"And now," he says, "how about a cup of coffee?"

———

The coffee shop in the hospital's shut this time of night – or rather the morning – but as luck would have it there's an all-night café about a minute's walk down the road. I slip out with Varga – the mortuary will just have to look after itself for now. There's every chance that one way or another this will be my last night at the hospital. Or with you. It still might be my last night anywhere.

Not that it's going to be if I can help it. To compound my list of procedural breaches for the night, I'd stashed my coat in an empty freezer drawer, and I'm wearing it now, one hand thrust into one of its deep pockets, holding onto the Roth-Steyr while Varga walks ahead of me. He keeps looking back at me, his hand in *his* coat pocket. In theory, he could probably take me out if he moved fast enough: I'm out of practice, after all. But he couldn't be sure I wouldn't get him too.

In any case, by the time we reach the café, I'm almost sure he's telling the truth about not wanting to kill me. None of which changes the fact that he did kill Tibor and Erick. I should hate him for that, shouldn't I? And yet, I don't. I should want to kill him too. But I don't.

———

After the Armistice was signed, the Black Eagles led us quite the merry dance, all through Central and Eastern Europe. In Britain, you think of the Armistice as the end of the Great War; the killing stopped at 11 am, November 11th 1918, and that was that. But you were on the winning side. East of France and Flanders, things were very different.

That was where the great land Empires – Austria, Germany, Russia and Turkey – were, and by 1918 every one of those had fallen apart. There were revolutions and counter-revolutions; there were new countries being born, tearing themselves free of their former masters, and often fighting among themselves, or even *with* themselves in bloody civil wars. It wasn't until 1923 and the Treaty of Lausanne that any kind of real stability came to the region, and even then it was tenuous. If you want to know why Fascism was such an easy sell in that part of the world and why so many people felt freedom and democracy were luxuries to be sacrificed, there's your first clue.

The Black Eagles scattered, and went from country to country. Part of it was to lose themselves in the chaos and part of it was in the hope of finding power – political office, military command, or just manpower – for their games. They had mixed success in the first aim, and better luck in the second. But in the course of trying to hunt down Varga and his pals, I saw the war and its aftermath in all its ugly detail. We went to Latvia and saw what had become of Riga: once the fourth-biggest city in the Russian Empire, now shattered and in ruins, half its population gone. Finland burst into civil war that killed a full one percent of its entire population. In Hungary, Count Károlyi's new liberal government was overthrown by Béla Kun's Communist revolution, which fought brief bloody wars with Romania and Czechoslovakia before in turn being overthrown. The Greeks invaded Anatolia and Thrace via the city of Smyrna, killing, burning and raping. They were beaten and driven back, wreaking more destruction in their retreat. The Turks fell upon Smyrna and burned it, killing thousands, adding to the victims of their earlier genocides. And so on, and so on, and so on. Death and destruction everywhere, vengeance heaped on vengeance for the crimes of history or for the recent savageries of war. None of it, none of it, made a single thing better that I could see.

It changed us all; Tibor's humour became less ebullient and more a brittle shield against the world. Erick, always quiet, became withdrawn to the point of silence. And me? I think Ulrich and I fought the same battle against ourselves, with different outcomes. The choice, in the face of such atrocity and suffering, was between feeling and duty; I chose one, he the other.

Tibor is dead and will never come back. Even if I salvage our relationship tonight, you'll never get to know him; the two people I love the most will never meet. Whether I kill Varga or not won't change that. I just want this over with. I want to return to my boring, mortal life.

I take a seat at the window and watch Varga as he goes to the counter and orders, then comes and joins me. "They're bringing it over," he says.

We sit, watching one another, aiming our guns at each other under the table. The tired-looking young woman behind the counter brings over a tray. On it are two mugs of black filter coffee, a bowl of sugar and an aerosol can of whipped cream. "*Einspänner*," says Varga, "to remind us of home. Not quite up to the standard of Sacher's or the Landtmann, but it will have to do."

"I always loved the Hawelka, myself," I say. "Oh, and the Grienstedl."

"Leon Trotsky's favourite," he smiled. "It closed, I'm afraid."

Even though I haven't been to Vienna in years, I'm saddened to hear it. "Really? When?"

"The summer of 2017. You only just missed it."

You suggested Vienna for our first holiday together, but I said no. We could have gone to Grienstedl's coffee house, where Tibor and I used to whisper our secrets to one another and giggle to ourselves. But we didn't, and now we never shall.

We drink our coffees. They aren't proper *Einspänners*; you serve *Einspänner* in a glass, and the coffee isn't as good as what they'd have served us in Vienna. Or perhaps that's just me looking back through rose-tinted glasses, to a time when I thought everything was better? I probably shouldn't go back to Vienna again, even if I ever get the chance. But it would be nice to have a proper *Einspänner* again, with a slice of *Linzer torte* or *Millirahmstrudel* to accompany it.

"I had trouble keeping my composure when I first saw you here," Varga says. He speaks softly, in German, and I slip into the same tongue to reply.

"You recognised me right away, then?"

"Yes." A smile. "You didn't."

"There's no easy way to say it, but… you've put on weight."

He laughs. "I know." The smile fades. "I'm sorry about your friends. Tibor Thököly, especially. I know you and he were close."

I nod. What am I supposed to say to that? Thank you?

"I swear to you, Countess, I didn't want to kill anyone. They didn't give me a choice."

I nod again. I want Tibor back alive again, so that I can shake him and demand to know what happened, why he didn't walk away too? A horrible thought occurs to me, that perhaps if I'd still been with the group, if I'd stayed a little longer, the two of us might have left together. That by the time any doubts set in, Tibor was alone except for the other hunters; no way of finding me, nowhere else to go. Not everyone can strike out on their own, especially when being part of some other group's a long-ingrained habit.

"I wasn't sure about you at first," he says. "I mean, when I saw you here, that first night—"

"When they brought Erick in, you mean?"

"Yes. Yes, after I killed him." He shrugs. "I was able to arrange things so that I took the case. So that I could control the investigation. It seemed safest."

"I see."

"You can imagine my surprise the first time I walked into the mortuary and saw you there."

Despite everything, I half-smile. "At least you recognised me."

"I had to look into you at some length to be certain you were what you appeared to be. I had heard stories you'd left the group, but it's hard to be certain."

"I suppose I should be glad you didn't dispose of me too."

A touch of irritation, mixed with sadness. "I told you, I didn't want to kill anyone. I was afraid I'd have to disappear again, but I eventually realised you were on your own and that the reports I'd heard about your leaving the *Falkenjaeger* were true. Erick, Tibor – they both came looking for me. I gave them the same choice I gave you tonight. They didn't take the opportunity." He looks agitated. "I don't know how I can convince you – I know it's near-impossible."

"I suppose the fact that I'm still alive is something of a clue," I admit. No getting around it – I flat-out failed to recognise Varga and it would have been the easiest thing in the world for him to waylay me afterwards and finish me too. "Unless of course you were hoping to get to Ulrich through me. He's the only one left now." I feel a twinge of fear – fear mixed with something else that I don't want to acknowledge, but reluctantly must: hope. "Or have you killed him too? Are we the last two left?"

Varga shakes his head. "I told you, I don't want to kill anybody. I don't know where he is, but I've no doubt he's out there somewhere. As I see it, I have three choices – I can kill him too, I can try to capture him and make him see reason, or I can run. Let Detective Inspector Charles Reeve die, and move on."

"True," I say. "But unless Ulrich has changed a lot, I wouldn't try capturing him."

"My thoughts too," he says. "But that isn't your problem, unless you want it to be." He drinks his coffee. "So, when was it you left?"

"Berlin," I say.

Tracking the Black Eagles through the chaos and intrigue of inter-war Europe, and then that of the war itself, was slow, ugly work. By 1945, I'd reached my limit for it.

"That's it for me," I told the others, as we sat in a burned-out third floor flat watching Russian tanks roll down the *Unter den Linden*. "I'm done."

Erick said nothing. I doubt he even heard me. He'd taken a bullet through the leg – one of the special kind – and Tibor had shot him full of morphine to deaden the pain. Ulrich's face flushed and he opened his mouth, but Tibor kicked him in the ankle. "Don't be such a silly cunt, Valerie," he said, and lit three cigarettes; he handed one to Ulrich and one to me, then nodded down at the body on the floor. "Think he's got any booze on him?"

Grumbling, Ulrich rooted through the pockets of SS *Standartenführer* Gertan Rust, formerly Lieutenant-Colonel Tasziló Czobor of the 9th Maros-Vásárhely Honvéd Hussars and the Black Eagles of the Crownland. Even with the city being blown apart around us, Czobor had put up one hell of a fight, wounding Erick and nearly killing the rest of us during the hour-long shootout we'd just ended.

In the end Tibor had kept him pinned down while Ulrich crept up on him, flushing him out into my line of fire. I'd emptied nearly a full magazine into Czobor, nearly cutting him in half, although I'd kept one bullet back for a *coup de grace*. Horváth would have been proud.

Ulrich wiped the blood off a crumpled silver hipflask, then gave it a shake. "You dented it, sister," he said, "but somehow you managed not to fuck it up completely."

Ulrich: he was, perhaps, the best of us in one sense: he was the perfect *Falkenjaeger*. He had been the first of the family to go to war: his regiment had been part of the Serbian Campaign, and he had come back from that a very different man. Colder. Emptier. All he spoke of was Duty, and the Empire. This life suited him: he was both dead and immortal now, and could be anyone he wanted for as long as he chose, then change identities when bored. But at the same time he was shackled to this task; that was the one constant in his existence, and he wouldn't really be free until it was done. And what would he be then? What was left? He was my twin, and yet his nature had grown so alien to me.

And I? What had I hidden from myself? I had learned that the role I'd fought so long and hard to prove worthy of didn't truly fit me. I was no more the steely avenger of the Habsburg Dynasty than I was the demure society lady. What was I then? The debauched hedonist of pre-war Viennese society, or something wholly different from anything I'd been before?

Ulrich uncapped the flask and took a swig, then made to throw it at me. He laughed when I flinched, and gave it to Tibor.

We'd all changed, but Tibor probably the least. He was still, of course, riotously gay, working his way ravenously through successive partners, although these debauches were carefully arranged and scheduled now, in order not to neglect our sacred mission. Now he drank, grimaced and handed me the flask."Careful," he said, "I think it might be aviation fuel."

He might well have been serious: some of those who'd walked the Gate sought out ever more extreme experiences, to test the nature of their limits. But Tibor had been joking; the flask's contents were alcohol, although I wasn't sure I wanted to know what it had been distilled from or its strength. It burned going down, and sent a flood of warmth through my body: that, just then, was good enough.

The tanks rumbled loudly outside, a seemingly endless stream. Dust and soot fell from the ceiling.

I screwed the top back on the flask. Erick was still gazing blankly, the cigarette hanging from his mouth almost burned down to the stub. Ulrich wouldn't look at me. Tibor glanced at Erick, too, then took the cigarette from his mouth and shook his head; I tossed the hip-flask back to him. "I'm serious," I said. "I'm done."

"Valerie," said Tibor, "you can't just walk away."

"Seems easy enough to me."

"You swore an oath," said Ulrich.

"Like you care," I snapped. "You just like killing."

"Oh, and you hate it. That's why you're so fucking proficient at it."

I shrugged. "I can do it if I have to. Not much of a way to spend your life, though, is it? Especially when you have forever."

"Yes," said Tibor, "we *do* have forever. Once the job's done, we can enjoy ourselves however we see fit. But until then—"

"Assuming we aren't killed in the process." I nodded at Czobor's corpse. "He damned near got us all."

"So?" said Ulrich. "We're soldiers. We have to do it."

"Why? You seriously think the Black Eagles are ever going to bring back the Empire now? Most of them are dead, and the ones we've found – how much interest did they have in it?"

Our little unit of seven – now four – had been issued with all the information the *Evidenzbureau* had managed to gather on those Black Eagles still at large, immortal or otherwise. We had minimal contact with other squads, who we knew only by codename to better protect one another from discovery if a mission went wrong – and only in order to exchange information on targets eliminated, losses sustained, new information acquired.

Of the eight Black Eagles we'd found and killed so far, two had been mercenaries, fighting wars for pay, while the others had left not only the Eagles' grandiose designs, but their military pasts, behind them. Czobor had been the only one still active in the empire-building stakes.

The most recent kill, before this one, had bothered me: in fact it had set me on the road to the decision I'd just made. The target had been a one-time Major in the Imperial-Royal *Landwehr,* Janos von Hortzweig zum Schengen. He'd settled in Paris, adopting a French identity and a flawless French accent, married and become a doting father to three children. He'd become a baker, of all things, and lived, as far as we could tell, as blameless a life as anyone could. By the time we caught up with him in July 1942, he'd been working with the French Resistance for eighteen months.

But we'd taken him off the street, bundled him into a Renault, driven him out into the countryside and interrogated him about his old comrades, promising him his life if he cooperated. Did he believe us? A desperate man will clutch at any rope. He'd told us all he could, but most of it was long out of date. It wouldn't have saved him anyway.

After von Hortzweig talked, we'd drawn straws to choose the executioner. At least I hadn't had to do that. I *did* actually draw the short straw, but Ulrich wasn't happy with the result. Another thing that pissed Ulrich off about me was that I'd actually killed more Black Eagles, one way or the other, than he or Tibor, and he saw no reason why I should have all the fun.

Yes, fun. That was how my brother thought now. He'd been part of the Army's campaign in Serbia before he'd walked the Gate; he'd never talk to me about what had happened, but it had changed him: he came back cold and hard and cruel, someone I no longer knew. He pushed me aside and put two rounds from his Frommer Stop pistol in the back of von Hortzweig's skull, just as he started to pray. The irony was that if Ulrich had wanted to cause me pain, he could have just stood back and watched me carry out the execution myself.

We buried von Hortzweig in a shallow grave. I mumbled a quiet prayer, so that the others wouldn't hear. Ulrich had wanted to go after von Hortzweig's family too. We didn't know if the Sindelar Gate's effects could be passed on; did we want his immortal offspring coming after us? But I'd drawn the line at infanticide, promising Ulrich a bullet in the leg (I wasn't quite ready for fratricide either) if he tried it; I was finding it harder and harder to sustain the ruthlessness Sergeant Horváth had sought to instil.

Von Hortzweig's death was the turning point, Louise: but as so often, it takes time before you finally make the change. Three years of denial, rationalisation and excuses. It might have finished earlier if we hadn't picked up the trail of two more Black Eagles in early

'43. Or, perhaps, without that I'd have vacillated even longer.

Tracking them down had been a welcome distraction at first. It had always been my speciality: even as a child I'd tended to become interested in things girls weren't supposed to like. So I'd learned very early on how to be patient and persistent, to ask questions without putting people on guard, to get access to books I wasn't supposed to read. That was how I'd become a woman who was valuable to the *Evidenzbureau*, and, ultimately, valuable to our team.

We first heard that Czobor, along with a Slovak Black Eagle called Lekaren, was in Portugal, working for the Salazar government. We found and killed Lekaren, but lost Albin in the process. We learned from Lekaren's papers that Czobor had moved on years before, assuming a new identity, and was now an SS officer. But to learn more, we'd have to enter Germany itself.

Crossing a continent in wartime isn't easy, especially when you're heading into the heart of a totalitarian state. And that was only the beginning: after that we had to assume fake identities, and find out what Czobor was calling himself now – all while ensuring we didn't arouse any suspicion and cause him to switch identities again. It took us nearly two years to find him, and only because Czobor hadn't really changed his spots: he was still in love with the idea of a Germanic Empire of one kind or another, and still blaming Jews, liberals, homosexuals et al for the world's ills. Now, as SS-*Standartenführer* Rust, he commanded an *einsatzgruppe* in *Reichskommisariat Ostland* – the Baltic States, Belarus and northeast Poland – exterminating Jews, Slavs and other 'undesirables'.

By the autumn of '44, the *Reichskommisariat* was collapsing, and Czobor relocated to the General Government, which controlled the rest of Occupied Poland. We reached there in early '45, but his unit was already falling back before the Russian advance. We'd spent our time avoiding both German and Russian forces, but we saw in detail the barbarity both sides had subjected the Poles – and the Jews – to. We found a concentration camp, abandoned by the Nazis, heaped with skeletal dead. Knowing Czobor had been a part of that process, I won't deny, made planning his death considerably easier.

We finally ran him to ground in Berlin. By then it was a city of ruins and corpses – bodies hung from lampposts, lynched by the Nazis for 'defeatism' in the face of the enemy, while raped and slaughtered civilians marked the Soviet advance. I'd already made my decision by then – the concentration camp had confirmed it. My whole life, or so it felt, had been in service of death, and it was a master I would serve no more. Czobor's, I'd decided, would be the last life I'd take.

"We can't be sure they've abandoned their plans," said Tibor. "The whole point was to work over the long-term."

"That isn't the point," snapped Ulrich. "We swore an oath to the Emperor. Hunt them down and kill them, every last one."

"Ulrich," I said, "I just don't give a fuck anymore."

He went white and clutched at his side; I didn't realise until Tibor grabbed his wrist to pinion him that Ulrich had been reaching for his gun. I'd been too exhausted and drained to act, and if not for Tibor, I'd have been dead at my own twin's hands. The last war, as I said, had done terrible things to Ulrich.

"That's enough," said Tibor, "both of you."

"The Emperor's dead," I said, "and so's the Empire."

"For God's sake, Val," Tibor said. He glanced to his right, but Erick was still staring into nowhere. I'm still sorry I never said a proper farewell to him.

"Even the Eagles know by now," I said, "that some things can't be restored."

That was when I left. Even for an immortal, it was safer to travel in groups to avoid captivity and pain, but I'd seen the look on Ulrich's face. As I ran down the ruined stairs I heard them struggling, and Ulrich shouting "Traitor! Coward! Traitor!" after me. I wasn't sure if Tibor would be able to hold him back. Or willing.

*That* was a painful thought; estrangement from Ulrich was bad enough, but the thought that Tibor might think of me the same way was unbearable. He might not have, of course, but I hadn't dared meet his eyes.

I disappeared into the ruined streets of Berlin, looking for places to hide and to evade the troops of either side. I managed, overall.

———

Varga is silent. "Were you there, too?" I ask.

He shakes his head. "Budapest, trying to hold off the Russians. But that meant fighting with the Germans and the Arrow Cross. And I'd... seen evidence of what they'd done to the Jews."

I raise my eyebrows. "I know," he snorts, "I know. But it's one thing to parrot that stuff. Quite another to see its ultimate conclusion. Anyway, I left soon after, before it was too late."

"Was that when you broke with the Eagles?"

"No. I left them long before that. I was the first to do so, in fact. I stayed in touch with a couple of them. But they're all gone now."

"All of them? Even Janacek?"

"Yep. Janacek killed himself back in '97."

The waste, the total fucking waste, of it all. "So what brought it on?" I ask. "You leaving, I mean?"

"God, Countess—"

"Valerie."

"Sorry?"

"Call me Valerie, Varga. I haven't been a Countess in a long time. And besides, I think we know one another well enough by now, don't we? In our way?"

He smiles. "I suppose we do. Valerie, then. As long as you call me Ferenc."

"All right."

We share a laugh. We should hate each other; we should be trying to kill one another. We don't. We aren't. I don't know how I feel, or am supposed to. I want to be home; I want to be with you.

"You know how it was then," Varga says. "The chaos, the violence. Revolutions, putsches, coups. And so much bloody slaughter. It's easy to kill, when you're young – to kill and kill. But as time goes on…

"There was no one great moment – it was cumulative. I saw the excesses of communist revolutionaries, of nationalists, and of loyalists to the old regimes, and realised I'd helped it all come to pass. You see before you a late convert to liberal democracy, I suppose."

"And now you're a policeman?"

"I'd brought chaos. The best amends I could make was to bring order. Chaos opens the door to madmen and dictators. All across Europe, thanks to us, they welcomed such people with open arms. I decided to do what I could. Once I felt reasonably sure I wouldn't be murdered by my ex-comrades, I went back to Hungary and joined the police. I had no love for Admiral Horthy and his ilk, but Hungary was my home and I wanted to..."

I wait.

"I didn't want to shape the destiny of nations," Varga says at last. "I just wanted to... to atone for what I'd done, try to make Hungary a peaceful place to live. Being a policeman meant cracking heads and keeping order, yes – but it can mean looking the other way, too, or bending the rules. I helped a lot of Jews escape the gas chambers, and I'm proud of that. After the war, I hoped to see my country become a democracy, but I had to clear out when the Russians came. I almost went back in '56 – lucky I didn't. I came to Britain a refugee, but a few changes of identity later, here I am, as British as they come. As far as everyone's concerned, anyway."

"And still a cop?"

"Turns out I'm good at it. It's a form of service. Gives some sort of meaning to life, I find."

I start to laugh, and can't stop. Varga frowns. I put my hands over my mouth, trying not to draw attention, although given that Varga and I are the only people here apart from the girl behind the counter it's hard to avoid doing so. I'm crying as I laugh, too, so I keep one hand over my mouth and wipe my eyes with a paper napkin.

At last, Varga smiles. "Yes, I suppose it is all rather absurd, isn't it?"

"Pointless is the word I was looking for. Your lot were supposed to be crusading for eternity, weren't you? Bring back the Empire, even if it took forever? And you lasted less than five years."

"I know. A bloody waste. All of it."

I'm not sure if he means the Sindelar Gate, or if he's looking all the way back to Mayerling and all that followed from that. Either will do. "So what happens now, Ferenc?"

"Between you and I? Nothing has to. I'm not fighting this war any longer."

"Nor am I. But what about Ulrich?"

Varga considers. "I'll move on, I think. Time to go somewhere else. Britain is… not as enjoyable a place to live as it once was."

"I know what you mean."

"And yet we've stayed."

"One gets used to things."

Varga smiles. "You're in love, Countess. That makes a place more appealing."

I feel cold at that, when I realise that you, too, were on the radar of this stupid fucking war. "I suppose it does."

He stands. "I'll say goodbye, then. Be well, Valerie." I nod.

"I'm sorry about Tibor."

"So am I."

"I truly didn't want to—"

"I know."

He nods. "Goodbye, then."

"Goodbye."

The door shuts behind him.

So. What do I do now? I can continue as before, if I want. I'd assumed tonight marked the end of my hospital job, but now it doesn't have to. Although I'll have to explain my way out of abandoning my post like that, assuming anyone's noticed...

But a job is a job, and one is easily changed for another. A love is considerably more important, and harder to replace. Or to sustain, once damaged by betrayal.

And while I want to say I haven't betrayed you, I know I have. From the first, really, I have: you've thought you were in love with me, but the person you loved didn't exist. Not really.

But I made you a promise, and I must keep it. I promised I would come straight to you and tell you everything, and so I will. I will.

In theory, I don't have to anymore. Things can go back to how they were, and I'd be astonished if I, having dealt in lies for so long, couldn't come up with a suitably convincing falsehood. But, quite simply, I don't want to. The prospect of dropping the lies and evasions, of being known at last by another mortal soul, is too lovely, too appealing, to refuse.

I drink the last of my coffee – Varga's makeshift *Einspänner* – slowly, steadily, trying to calm and compose myself. All of a sudden, I want an *Einspänner*, a real *Einspänner* and a *Linzer torte*; I want to enjoy them in the Hawelka café with you. You and I in Vienna: I want that, now, more than anything. Take you back to where it began.

I stand up. I'm actually excited. No more dread at the prospect of telling the truth; I'm allowing myself, dangerously, to hope – something I really shouldn't do – that this mightn't be the end of us. It really isn't much of a hope – so many obstacles, so many dangers – and perhaps the appeal is also in the potential destruction of everything between us, an end to the effort of maintaining it.

But either way, I will cope.

I have survived far worse, after all.

---

I go back for my things and drive home, trying as I go to decide where to begin, what order to put things in. Or perhaps it's better to let it just spill out. Perhaps, or perhaps not. At the beginning, at least, surely I need to calculate what I say and do, so that you'll actually believe me. Eliminate the tedious process of your humouring me; begin by proving what I say.

There's so much to tell, and when I start, how will I stop? Even now, there are things I want to hide from you – or one thing, at least. After all these years, it isn't the human lives I've taken that bother me, although I take no pride in the Black Eagles I've killed. No, what preys on me and shames me still, what I'd really still rather you never knew about, is the death of that nameless, sweet-faced little dog in Budapest all those years ago, killed by the pistol in my shoulder-bag. I'd rather hide that from you, if I can. But the trouble with telling the truth, after so long spent lying, is that once you start it's hard to stop.

---

How can I explain the Sindelar Gate to you, what it was like to walk it? How do I even begin to describe the experience of becoming immortal?

The Gate stood, officially, in Dr Sindelar's laboratory, but I'm not sure that 'laboratory' is really the right word. It was located in a forest near the Sulm Valley; all I know about the place – we were driven there, blindfolded, one night in mid-October, 1918 – was that it was underneath a mound in the centre of a huge forest clearing. My initial impression, once Horváth told us to remove the blindfolds, vague though it was in the glow of the moon and stars and the headlights of the trucks, was of a tumulus: it had a perfect, regular shape, which Nature doesn't usually provide.

Sappers had carved a tunnel into the side of the mound, supported by wooden uprights. Electric lights had been rigged inside, and in their glow I saw worms writhing away from our approach on either side of the duckboards on the floor. At the end of the tunnel was a small chamber containing an electric winch, attached to an elevator cage. The cage hung in space, above a shaft leading down.

"Halt," said Horváth. "Stand easy." He drummed his fingers on the butt of his gun. "All right," he said, "Three at a time. Von Bradenstein-Vršovci, other von Bradenstein-Vršovci, and Thököly – you first."

Ulrich, Tibor and I climbed into the lift, which was basically a wooden platform with steel mesh strung between metal supports on three sides, and then Horváth nodded to the sapper standing by the winch. There was a whirr, and the lift sank down.

That was my very last sight of Sergeant Sándor Horváth; he stood, his hands clasped behind his back, watching us sink from sight. His face was impassive – not mocking at all, for once. There might have been respect, or even sadness, in it.

Raw earth walls, glistening with moisture under the electric lights, gave way to bare black stone.

The air grew colder, till it was bitter. And then the narrow shaft walls opened out. There was an instant of blackness so total that it was terrifying in its intensity, before the electric lights strung along the roof of the underground chamber swept the darkness away, and I was never so glad of the invention as I was then. I don't think I ever have been since.

The cage sank down, wobbled to a halt and was still.

Half a dozen soldiers marched to meet us. One motioned for us to get out of the cage, so we did. The others in our training group arrived, three at a time, and we all stood waiting.

I've described where we'd arrived as a chamber, but it would be more accurate to call it a cavern. It was a natural formation of some kind, a huge cave hollowed out far beneath the barrow.

A small, rat-like man in a white coat came forward to greet us. Oiled blond hair and beady blue eyes in a pale, bony face. "Welcome," he said. "I'm Dr Hynek Sindelar."

"A pleasure," said Tibor.

"Indeed. And my congratulations to you all. Your training has been arduous, I know. But we must have the right people. Please, come this way."

I disliked Sindelar on sight: there was something greasy and low about him. It didn't help, of course, to know that it was thanks to him that the Black Eagles had become immortal in the first place: he was helping us only because of a combination of bribes and threats. Not exactly a firm foundation for trust. But however Sindelar had made his discovery, I suspect he would have offered it to the first bidder. He had no great loyalty to any iteration of the Empire, or anything else that I could see.

We followed him across the cavern to the darkness at its edge. As we neared it I realised that this darkness, which I'd taken to be the outer wall of the cavern, was simply an area that was not as yet illuminated. A table swam into view in the muzzy twilight at the periphery of the lit area; on it was a power switch. Nearby was a row of chairs, which Sindelar motioned to. "Please disrobe," he said.

"I'm sorry?" said Tibor.

"Disrobe. No metal, no fabric, no wood can pass through the Gate. Only warm, living flesh. Naked flesh." He was looking at me when he said that, and I was sorely tempted to slap his face. I resisted. Just.

"Your superiors have briefed you on the risks?" he said.

"They did," I said. "They said it was an experimental procedure, and there were risks of failure, in a small number of cases."

"Ah yes. A small percentage. Not as small as I would like, of course. These things never are."

"Er… how small, exactly?" Tibor asked.

"Barely in double figures." Sindelar coughed. "Well. In double figures, yes, but certainly far less than fifty per cent." He coughed again. "Somewhat less."

There was a silence. It would be fair to say that the level of risk may have been slightly understated.

"So," said Sindelar, "as I said – please disrobe." He licked his lips.

I took off my clothes, and so did the others. In fairness to Sindelar, it wasn't just me he was staring at. Lord alone knows what his sexuality was. Frustrated virgin, possibly. It wasn't hard to believe he'd never had intercourse in his life.

I concentrated on the task of folding my clothes – a plain pike-grey military uniform, slightly re-tailored to fit the female form – and putting them on one of the chairs, tucking the boots neatly together underneath. I could feel Sindelar's eyes on me. To this day, I still regret not slapping him.

"Atten*tion*!" called Sindelar, and giggled. We all stood up straight. I could see my breath. I very much wanted to cover myself with my hands, and for that very reason I didn't. I wouldn't give him the satisfaction.

Goose-pimples rose on my skin in the cold. Sindelar studied us, smiling. Tibor rolled his eyes, struck a coy pose, fluttering his eyelashes, and blew him a kiss. I couldn't hold back a snort of laughter. Even Ulrich chuckled. Sindelar went red and clenched his fists, then smirked and licked his lips. "We'll see how amusing you find matters shortly. There's no sense delaying further. Behold!"

Sindelar went to the table and threw the switch. Lights flickered on, illuminating the remainder of the cavern, and at last we saw the Sindelar Gate.

First, I suppose, I should describe the Gate itself. It was about eighteen feet tall and ten wide, built of plain grey stone blocks, unadorned except for a dark blue crystal, resembling a huge sapphire, set into each one. The inside of the gate was silvered and polished. A raised walkway, also silvered, led through it, for ten feet on either side.

Around the walkway stood thirteen things in black, hooded robes. Things, yes, because they couldn't have been men: all but one of them were eight feet in height. Six stood on one side of the walkway, six on the other and the thirteenth – taller than the rest, almost twelve feet high – at the very end. They were as thin as they were tall, and draped in dusty, purplish-black robes that hung loosely on them. Their sleeves overlapped their clasped hands, hiding them from view, and their cowls drooped over their faces like wilted blooms. My first thought was that Sindelar had, for some unknown reason, placed a set of giant mannequins around the Gate, but as one they raised and turned their heads towards us, making no sound other than the shifting of their robes.

"My assistants," said Sindelar, and giggled. "Now, please pay attention. Very shortly, we'll begin. When we do, you must follow my instructions precisely. That shouldn't be difficult, as all any of you will need to do is to get on the walkway and – well, walk." He giggled again. "Simple, no? However, please be aware of this: once the ritual has begun, you must not attempt either to leave the walkway or to move backwards. To do so would be fatal. I am not joking, my friends."

He wasn't smiling any more, or even ogling us. He was sombre and deadly serious. "All you need to do, as I say, is to put one foot in front of the other until you're through the Gate and have reached the walkway's end. No matter what you experience. Do this and, all being well, you will have attained that which many people have desired but very few achieved: physical immortality. If not... well, I've only recently finished hosing down the walkway after the last failure. Do any of you have any questions before we begin?"

"What exactly is going to happen?" I said.

I expected a mocking reply – *you'll walk through the Gate, have you already forgotten what I told you?* – but Sindelar surprised me. "When you enter the Gate, you will no longer be entirely in our world. You will enter a different domain."

"What domain?"

"It has many names. The point is this: the forces that operate within that domain will alter you. Subtle but profound changes to your physical body will result. But this is the important part: the Gate works because you will, in effect, be in *both* realms simultaneously. Both this world and the other will be trying to claim you. The changes caused by the Gate come from this – you might say – tug of war effect. This is why you must, at all costs, maintain forward motion. If the other domain were to claim you *in toto*—"

"The results would be fatal," said Ulrich. "Yes?"

"Only if you were fortunate," Sindelar replied. "Are there any further questions?"

I was hoping there would be – having finally reached this point I now wanted to delay the moment as long as I possibly could – but there were none. "Very well, then, we shall begin. You should walk in single file, and leave at least three paces between one another. Proceed in whatever order you see fit."

I looked around the cavern. The soldiers had regrouped to block our path to the lift. No-one who backed out now could be permitted to leave, possessing as they would that dangerous combination of too much knowledge and insufficient resolve for their masters' liking.

"I'll go first," I said. Cowardly on my part, perhaps, but I didn't want to see what happened to Ulrich or Tibor before I made my attempt. I had no idea what that would do to my resolve.

"As you wish, Countess."

"Me next," said Ulrich.

"That leaves me to bring up the rear," said Tibor.

"Thought that was your preferred position," I grinned.

"It is better to give than to receive."

Sindelar breathed in sharply through his nose. "This is a serious matter."

"Apologies," said Tibor. "Do we begin?"

Sindelar glowered at us both, then stole a nervous glance at the Gate – or rather, at its silent guardians. "Yes," he said, and gestured towards the walkway. "Get into position, but await my signal before stepping on the walkway."

"Will do."

"And remember, Countess – maintain forward motion at all times until you have left the walkway again."

"All right," I said. "But let's get on with this before my nipples fall off."

Sindelar went bright red. "Valerie," muttered Ulrich, looking disgusted. Tibor sniggered.

Sindelar turned away from us, moving off to the side, and then said something to the tallest Monk, the one standing at the far end of the walkway. Although I knew most of the Empire's various languages and a smattering of many outside its border – it came in handy at the *Evidenzbureau* – I had no idea what he said. I assume it was either a command or a request. It was hard to tell from the tone, because the language's rhythm and inflections were unlike anything I'd previously encountered. But after he said it, the tallest of them raised its arms and began to speak in a dry hoarse rustling whisper that sounded like the movements of a huge insect. The other Monks began speaking too, and I thought of a horde of cockroaches and centipedes and worse crawling and slithering over one another. I wasn't afraid, as such; there was something beyond fear in how my body and psyche responded.

The Monks, as well as speaking, now began to move. Nothing much; they rocked slightly in position, their heads nodded, and their arms moved as though they were making small, complicated gestures with their hands, but there was something about those movements which, like their voices, put me in mind of something inhuman and repellent. *Repellent*, in fact, is the best word I can find to describe them; I simply wanted to be as far away from the Monks as I could. But I had volunteered for this, it was far too late to back out even if I wanted, and, after having jumped through all of Horváth's hoops, having proven myself over and again to possess the courage, the intelligence, the dedication and the steel for this task, was I really going to back out now, like some society belle with an attack of the vapours?

The whispers grew in volume, and continued on and on. As they became louder, I made out individual words, although their meaning was a mystery – it was the same unknown language Sindelar had instructed them in. Where had he found these people – if they *were* people – I hadn't asked him, and it was too late now, but it wouldn't have surprised me to learn that the Gate had been buried in the barrow, and that he'd found them there with it, sleeping a sleep that he'd disturbed. What was happening here seemed to owe less to science than it did to something far older and darker.

At first I thought a light was being reflected in the Gate's sapphires, but when I turned and looked I saw no sign of one. The faint, weak flashes of light from the gems grew more frequent and intense, until I saw that the glow was coming from inside them. Soon they began to shine.

The chanting grew louder and louder, and next the silvered interior of the gate began to shine – again, it was as though light was reflecting off it. Glowing strands of light, like the kind you see in a Van der Graaf generator, began to dart and writhe between the metallic surfaces. The chanting grew louder still.

"Now, Countess," said Sindelar. There was no time to think; I treated it as an order, and I'd learned to respond to those immediately and without question.

I stepped onto the walkway, and had to clench my teeth to avoid yelping out loud; the silver was so cold that the soles of my feet stuck to it.

It was no more half a dozen paces than to the Gate itself, but I could already understand why people faltered. I reminded myself only just in time to take the second step without a pause. Then second step, and then a third. By that point, the sparks that leapt between the inner surfaces of the gate had blurred into a hazy blue and violet glow; I couldn't see the cavern beyond it, or the end of the walkway, but took a fourth step nonetheless. I felt my skin prickle as I neared the Gate. There was a sensation like static electricity, raising my body hairs.

I took a fifth step; the sixth would take me through the Gate. *Constant forward motion*, I reminded myself, and then walked into the blue-violet haze.

I'd once received an electric shock, and felt something similar then, although several orders of magnitude greater in intensity, along with a sensation both of searing heat and excruciating cold – as if I'd somehow been both burned by fire and buried in ice simultaneously. I very nearly froze where I stood, but managed to remember Sindelar's instructions and take another step.

The haze dissipated, and I was in freefall.

A kind of radiant darkness surrounded me, by which I mean I was in a void of utter blackness, and yet I could see. And I was not alone. There were – *things* – there.

There was no up, no down, no back, no forward – but Sindelar had said I must maintain forward motion, maintain it at all costs. How could I do that when I didn't even know what forward *was*?

Keep walking, no matter what. I was still myself. I still had legs and feet. Didn't I? It felt hard to be sure – everything felt so alien, and so numb. Unable to feel anything, there was no way of knowing.

I began walking anyway, or what I hoped was walking. And the sensation of freefall ceased. That was the only indication that I was making progress, so I continued.

Then I remembered I could still see, and looked down at myself. I saw my legs, moving regularly as if in motion, but they seemed unnaturally long. God knew to what extent I was able to trust my perceptions here; I looked up again. I could make out movement in the blackness, and I knew that the sensation of freefall I'd initially experienced had marked my descent towards that movement.

I couldn't make out *what* was moving as such. Have you ever peered into a beach-pool, and seen the movement of those small, sand-coloured fishes and transparent shrimps? With practice you can get some idea of what sort of creatures they are, but until then they're just movement without form. This was the same, except that these creatures were far larger and I knew that if I fell amongst them I would cease to exist in any meaningful sense.

Thankfully, as I continued to walk, my sense of proximity to those entities, whatever they were, receded. Even so, I knew I wasn't alone, and had no idea where, if anywhere, the exit from this void might be.

Most of the people who'd passed through the Gate had come out the other side. Or half, at least. I had to remember that. Unless Sindelar had lied. What if no-one had done so yet? What if every volunteer had walked into the Gate and never re-emerged, but he was still sending them, insisting that eventually it must work? Had he trapped me here forever? I mustn't think like that. I must believe that there was a way out, and that I would find it. I only needed to keep walking. *Maintain forward motion.* Surely then I'd find an escape. I had to believe that.

There was no distance or direction here, and nor was there any sense of time. I was suddenly convinced that I'd been here for months, even years. But I mustn't think of that, either. I must simply continue to walk. One foot in front of the other. Although direction was meaningless now too. I was no longer sure if I was moving my legs and feet correctly. I might be walking sideways or backwards, or kicking my legs as if swimming. I was tempted to look, but didn't. I was no longer sure I'd recognise forward motion if I saw it. I was no longer sure I would even recognise my legs, or any other part of my body. Everything felt alien and wrong. If you've ever performed an action so many times that it's lost its meaning, to the point that you're no longer certain of anything about it, you might understand. Not only was I afraid of how strange and distorted my body might now appear if I looked at it, I was no longer certain that I knew how it *should* appear, if what I thought I knew was the truth or a fantasy that I'd recalled. I mustn't look. If I did I might stop walking, or convince myself that I was doing it wrong. *At all costs maintain forward motion.* If this *was* forward motion. I had to believe that it was. This was why Sindelar had instructed us as he had, because we mustn't lose sight of that one simple goal.

I wondered if Ulrich had entered the Gate yet, or Tibor. I wondered how far behind me they were, and how they were coping. Perhaps they'd lost their battle with the void already. Perhaps they were already gone.

One foot in front of the other. Keep walking.

Colour! I could see colour in the void, something other than the shining dark. There was something red, and I began to regain my sense of direction. It was ahead of me, ahead and to the left, and as I continued to walk it drew closer. I couldn't discern its size, not then – I was uncertain of the distance, the range.

But as I continued to walk, not only did the red thing grow close, but it seemed to accelerate towards me. It grew as it did: at first I'd thought it might be roughly the size of a cow, then a car, then of a bus. And then I realised it was larger still.

It spread out below me as I walked, its surface turning. It was as though I was walking on a gigantic ball the size of the Moon, even of the earth itself. It was red. Red and purple. And brown. And tan. And white. It was, you see, composed of millions upon millions of interwoven threads, stretched-out and glistening and pulsating. It was alive. And it was screaming.

I didn't hear the screams so much as I felt them. When I looked away from it I saw at least half a dozen more of them at various distances from me in the firmament of the void. It wasn't alone. I hoped the reason I could suddenly see them was that I was progressing towards the end of my journey, and not because they had scented prey.

I looked down again towards the turning scarlet surface below me, studiously trying to avoid looking at my own body, fearful of what might have become of it, searching for any sign of hostile intent. I saw none, but what I did observe was far worse.

In one patch on the surface of the red thing, the threads were in motion. They unknotted, unravelled, thin tendrils spilling out into the void. For a second I feared they were some form of pseudopods, groping in search of food, but instead they recombined and formed the shape of an outstretched, grasping hand.

Another patch of the red thing writhed, unknotted and recombined. This time it didn't extend far from the surface, but shaped itself into a screaming face. The tendrils comprising the eyes writhed and shifted, changing colour, so that there were whites and irises. Blue irises. That was when I recognised the face: one of my fellow volunteers, a Carinthian boy called Josef.

The hand stretched out towards me. I think it was attempting to solicit help, but I don't believe I or any other human being could have done anything to aid or even kill whatever Josef had now become. And if it succeeded in grasping me, nothing good could come of it. *Maintain forward motion at all costs*: I couldn't do that with the red thing hanging from my leg like a plant-sized ball and chain.

I had no idea how to manoeuvre in the void, and if I tried I might lose my way (assuming I was travelling in the right direction to begin.) But Josef could only exert so much control over his material: as his hand tried to reach farther out, the strands that comprised it began to snap, retracting into the bulk of the red thing. Within seconds the whole hand had unravelled and fallen back. Only the screaming face remained, and as I watched even that was reabsorbed. The eyes were the last to go.

I looked ahead and continued to walk. The other red masses loomed larger; they didn't impinge on me as Josef had, and I avoided looking at them too closely. I didn't want to see how many of them there were. I might realise that my worst suspicions had been correct and that, whatever Sindelar had said, no-one entering the Gate had re-emerged.

I passed through the last of the red masses. Soon they were receding behind me. I didn't look back. There was, apart from anything else, something else to attract my attention now: in the distance, I thought I saw something: a single pinprick in the blackness of the void, a tiny, luminous speck. I thought, or perhaps hoped, that it was the same blue and violet colouration as the haze that had filled the Sindelar Gate.

I began to walk a little faster, although the blue spark stubbornly remained the same size. Maintain forward motion; that was all I could do. It occurred to me that Dr Sindelar hadn't briefed us on what to expect in here. Perhaps he'd feared he wouldn't be believed, or that the knowledge would fatally undermine our morale. Or perhaps – that horrible suspicion emerged again – nobody had made it through the Gate to tell the tale.

I clenched my fists and quickened my pace, telling myself that even if no-one else had, I would be the first to do so. But the blue spark remained as distant as ever.

And then I sensed movement in the dark.

As before, I could not, precisely, see what was there; I only recognised that something in the darkness, or perhaps the darkness itself, was in motion. I wanted to believe that my approach was startling them away, but I knew that wasn't the case; my approach, in fact, had awoken them. I could only close my eyes and continue – *maintain forward motion, maintain forward motion* – and hoped I could pass through them unmolested.

That was not to be.

The first of them seized me, and even when I opened my eyes and screamed into the void – making no sound, no sound at all – I couldn't see what it was, or be sure what part of it was holding onto me. A tentacle, a claw, a hand? I don't know. What I did know was that it had… penetrated me. And yes, I use that word exactly. It felt exactly as it sounds: a violation.

And yet I do not mean that it had forcibly entered my vagina, mouth or anus, nor yet that it had cut into me like a knife. Rather it *sank* into me, as though I were composed of liquid, and moved within.

Another limb, appendage, whatever it was, flowed through my skin – and then another, and another. Their pseudopods trailed through my guts, toyed with valves of my heart, stirred my brains like soup. They were in my eyes, my ears, my hair and skin, my lungs, my blood, the marrow of my bones.

By that point, I was convinced I was about to suffer the same fate as Josef, unravelled into a million miles of still-living, screaming fibres, to suffer through eternity. But somehow, I remembered to keep moving my legs. *Maintain constant forward motion; maintain constant forward motion:* I did that, even as I felt the Void-things that had invaded me begin to pull me apart.

I shut my eyes; if I couldn't see it, perhaps it wouldn't be real. If I kept walking, I might stand a chance. The agony of what they were doing was sudden and white, infinite and absolute. Had I stopped? I was vaguely aware of doing something, but I couldn't tell what. I had to walk. I had to walk.

I felt the Void-things pull me apart, and I felt them alter me. We didn't know about DNA back then, of course, but I wouldn't be surprised to learn that the intricate double-helix code that dictated who and what I was had been unwound and rewritten. Why they did it, I don't know. Because Sindelar, or the Monks, had bent them to their will? For their own amusement? Or simply because it was what they did?

I had no idea what they were doing, what I was becoming or – as I've said – whether I was in motion or not, but I was at least aware that their task was nearing completion. The pain had reached its zenith and was now beginning to fade, and the sensations I'd felt while they were unmaking me were beginning to reverse themselves. I took some comfort in that: no doubt I'd been screaming, to the extent that the void permitted me to, but I wasn't any more. Unlike Josef, whose torment had seen unending. But then, I didn't know what I'd become: when I did, I too might begin to shriek.

I was fairly certain now that I was still walking, so I continued to do so. At length the pain disappeared, and there was only the sensation of their – *appendages* – inside me, still probing and stirring, though now with no real intent. Last-minute inspections maybe, or a craftsman stroking a job well-done.

Then one by one, they pulled out of me, leaving me shockingly empty. But they were gone, and I was myself alone, whatever that might now be.

The void was still there; so was the blue spark. But it was a spark no longer: it was now a square of blue-violet light the approximate shape and size – if I was remembering my life before entering the Gate correctly – of my thumbnail.

I was getting closer, and the Void-things were gone.

I still didn't dare look at myself. I didn't want to know. If I did, and stopped moving, I might be trapped in the void forever like Josef and the rest. If I had been transfigured into something monstrous and obscene, then at least they might kill me out of mercy or revulsion if I made it out the other side.

Always assuming that I *could* die; I might become some horrible, agonised thing, turned inside out but incapable of perishing. The worst of all worlds. But there was no way to be certain now. I'd known the risks, I told myself – although had anyone, even Sindelar, truly understood them? The Monks might; I had, I have, no idea where they came from, but it's not impossible the void had been their home.

The thumbnail of light was now the size of my palm – the size my palm had been before the Gate. I must stop myself thinking like that. Forward. Forward. Forward.

The light was now the size of a human head. Then bigger. Bigger. I now felt as though I were being pulled towards it. Whatever forces existed in the void itself had less and less of a hold on me.

It was my height now, then taller: the height and width of the Sindelar Gate. There were blocks of stone around its edges, set with sapphirelike gems that glowed with an inner light. The inside of the gateway shone silver. I was no more than three paces away now; I took a step, then another, and the same prickling of the skin, as if from static electricity, that I'd felt when about to step through the Gate returned.

And then I stepped through.

A jolt like an electric shock, a simultaneous sensation of searing heat and searing cold, and then the air of the cavern hit me like a blast of wind, almost tipping me back through the Gate. I lurched forward, bare feet sticking even more than they had previously to the icy surface of the walkway.

Shouts, screams, cacophony: after the silence of the void every sound in the cavern was deafening. "Keep walking, Countess! Keep walking!" shouted a voice. It was Sindelar's.

I was out, I was through – except that I wasn't. I could feel something tugging at me. The Gate still clung to me. Its pull was weak but if I didn't resist it, it would yank me back in, and I would not emerge a second time.

I only had ten feet left to traverse. That's nothing, is it? I'd gone slowly on my way in, but only from fear of what awaited me. But I was past the worst now. No reason to move slowly. Except that I felt so weak, my limbs so shaky, almost boneless. Oh God, what had I become? Had it changed me into something monstrous?

I had better not look down. If what I saw shocked me into faltering, that would be the end of me. But my legs almost gave out. I stumbled and as I did I looked down, five feet from the end of the walkway, and screamed.

My legs were thick, gelatinous trunks of bloody slime. Hunks of their substance slid off as I walked to splatter onto the walkway. I swayed, and the Gate pulled at me.

"No! Countess, keep walking! All will be well! All will be well! Only maintain forward motion!"

I heaved myself forward in a final stagger towards the end of the walkway. As I did, more slime fell away and I realised that it was only a thick coating – one, in fact, that covered me from head to foot – and beneath it was I was still myself.

After a fashion.

My legs had always been long and lean, but now they were skin and bone. Broomstick lengths of knotted wood, with discoloured parchment stretched across them. My feet looked massive and grotesque in comparison.

I stumbled off the end of the walkway and lost my balance, sticking my arms out to break my fall. The impact was agonising, jarring, and I was afraid bones had been broken. But that wasn't as bad as seeing how equally emaciated my arms were. My hands were claws. I rolled away from the walkway, too weak to stand again; more slime sloughed off, exposing my torso. My stomach was concave, sinking inwards as if to reach my backbone; my ribs showed through the skin, and my pelvis was like a bowl. My breasts were shrivelled pouches; I resembled a thing made of pipe-cleaners, a mockery of the woman who'd walked into the Gate, and I heard a terrible wail and realised it was my own voice.

"Countess!" I heard Sindelar shout.

Something plopped to the ground in front of me. More slime, but a different colour. A sort of reddish colour, but not the red of blood. It was the colour of my hair.

I fumbled at the liqueous clot, trawled through the slime with shaking fingers and peered at what I held up to my face. Yes: it was my hair. I touched my scalp and my fingers slithered over smooth, hairless skin: more slime, thick with hair, splattered on the floor. I found one hank of hair still attached to my scalp, but it came away at my touch.

I cried out – in shock, horror and in pain, because agony now erupted from every joint in my body. My stomach heaved, my bowels and bladder failed and every breath burnt my lungs. My mouth was full of blood, and small, hard things. I spat: blood splashed the cavern floor and shining in it, yellow-white and whole, were my teeth, roots and all. I screamed again.

"Countess! Countess! All will be well, all will be well." Sindelar was kneeling beside me. "These effects are temporary. The loss of hair and teeth. They will grow back in days. You will regain your weight and health. You have my word." There was neither mockery or lechery in his voice. Not that my appearance would arouse the latter. "Fetch a blanket!" he called. He glanced upwards and bowed his head.

I followed his gaze. I had forgotten the Monks. The thirteenth one, the tallest, stood only feet away from me. Even close to, the being's robes hid its true appearance – their hem puddled on the floor, their sleeves overlapped and the cowl hung down to cover the face. I presumed it to be vaguely human-shaped, but beyond that, I decided, it was better not to know.

A blanket was placed around my shoulders, and I crawled aside. The blue-violet haze flickered inside the Gate, and a second emaciated, slime-covered figure came staggering out. I'm still not sure how I knew that it was Ulrich, but I did. I was convinced he was about to collapse and be yanked shrieking back into the void, but like me before him, he reached the end of the walkway and collapsed onto the stone floor. Moaning, coughing, shedding hair and slime and teeth, he crawled to me, and Sindelar draped a blanket round him too.

Fifteen of us, in all, had entered. All the group that Horváth had trained over those weeks. Soon, Tibor came out. Like Ulrich, like me, he was monstrously emaciated. After the war I would see identical skeletal scarecrow shapes when I was shown pictures of the Armenian men, women and children the Turks had death-marched into the Syrian desert; and, of course, less than half a century later, I'd see them again, in footage of Auschwitz and Belsen. I'd see them, too, in pictures from Serbia. Civilians who'd starved to death, thanks to the depredations of our own glorious Habsburg Army.

The Empire did monstrous things in Serbia, terrible things, atrocities. Had I know about them, would I still have joined the *Falkenjaeger*? I'd like to tell myself not, but perhaps I'm just deluding myself. The ability to rationalise any obscenity may be one of humanity's defining traits. I never knew what role Ulrich had played in the Serbian Campaign; I never asked him. I don't know if he would ever have told me, anyway. Perhaps I was afraid to hear, even at the time. Sometimes I wonder if we lost our souls in the Sindelar Gate; sometimes I wonder whether Ulrich had still, by then, had one to lose.

"How many?" whispered Sindelar, looking up at the thing that towered over us. For answer, it raised a huge bluish-coloured hand. The hand had too many digits, ending in curved, yellow-white talons. It held up five of them in all.

"Five," said Sindelar. He sounded disbelieving and ecstatic. "Five!"

The thing seemed to consider, then held up a sixth.

Erick stumbled out next, then Mathias, who would die in Istanbul in 1927. We watched the Gate, shivering under our blankets; just as it seemed there would be no sixth arrival, the blue and violet haze flickered once more, and something flopped onto the walkway.

I may have screamed, but in all honesty it's hard to tell. I know I tried, but I'm not sure what sound came out. Everyone else in the cavern seemed to be screaming too, even Sindelar, so I doubt I would have been able to hear myself.

The thing that began to claw its way along the silver walkway, with appendages that still vaguely resembled hands, had been turned inside out and… re-woven. Its new body was horribly long, continuing to drag itself from the void even as the fumbling hands neared the walkway's end. For all I know, it might have begun life as more than one person.

It had hands, but no face. No eyes. It was screaming though, or attempting to. The screaming sounded muffled. It may not have had a mouth, either. I have no idea which of us it had been.

Sindelar shouted orders. "Kill it!" he shouted. "For God's sake, kill it!"

The thing heard him, at least, and flailed blindly at the air around it with its arms, to fend off any attacks, before having to scrabble at the surface of the walkway again: its body still hadn't fully emerged from the Gate. The thing, still howling its muffled howl, made a last effort to drag itself over the edge of the walkway. But an officer and four men ran up, all clutching Steyr-Hahn pistols. The slides snapped back, and the malformed, asymmetrical lump that served the thing for a head whipped to and fro at the sound. "Aim!" shouted the officer.

The thing's arm shot outwards, extending like a length of boneless rubber; the clawed hand at the end latched onto the officer's throat and ripped it away. He fell to his knees, blood spraying through his fingers, and his men opened fire.

A Steyr-Hahn's magazine holds eight bullets; with four men standing by the walkway that meant thirty-two rounds were emptied into that inside-out, vermiform body in seconds. Blood, slime and other, half-solid matter erupted in all directions. The thing howled, and at one point the scream became unmuffled and exploded out of it at its fullest, most terrifying volume – presumably one of the bullets had torn something in its body to serve the purpose of a mouth. But still it thrashed, even when the guns were empty, and its arms, still elongating, flailed about in search of prey or handholds.

Dr Sindelar was, by now, gibbering some kind of prayer. The soldiers were reloading frantically, all except one who snatched up the officer's gun. Braver or stupider than the rest, he stepped forward, aimed at the thing's head and opened fire.

He didn't jump back from the flailing claws, but fell to one knee instead, still firing. His comrades had reloaded too now, but the thing had already collapsed and grown still. Even so, they kept shooting it as it was pulled back along the walkway and sucked back into the violet haze that filled the Sindelar Gate, leaving a trail of blood and slime, the officer's corpse and a scattering of empty cartridges.

I slumped forward on my hands and knees, but even they couldn't support me. The others – Ulrich and Mathias, Tibor and Erick – were already prone on the floor. The Monk, looming over us, raised its arms aloft in blessing or exultation as my own arms gave out, so I collapsed to the floor with the rest and we grovelled before it, as though it were our god.

Recovery was surprisingly fast: within the first forty-eight hours my teeth had begun to regrow, pushing through my raw and bloody gums with no shortage of agony. By the third day my body hair had begun to sprout again. I ate ravenously and almost incessantly, rapidly regaining the weight that I'd lost. By the fourth day my teeth were fully restored – including one I'd been missing before I walked the Gate – and my hair was at half its original length; within a week, I was indistinguishable from the woman who'd walked into it.

Outwardly, at least.

That week would be the longest period of recovery I would ever require again. Since then I haven't known a day's illness, and most physical injuries heal in seconds. It's the minor cuts and bruises that take longest to mend, funnily enough: whatever the Gate did to me, whatever it is in me that reacts to damage done, it responds the fastest to the greatest trauma. I could be cut in half or have my head literally blown off by a shell – in fact there's no *could be* about it, I've suffered both fates and recommend neither, immortality or no – and a new head would regrow in seconds, or a new lower half of my body develop (the old one withering and crumbling away) but a papercut, or a nick from shaving my legs? I'd heal no faster than you, Louise.

But (and not for the first time, I know, my patient love), I digress.

When we had recovered, we were assigned to our unit. Tibor, Ulrich, Erick, Mathias and I were introduced to two other survivors of the Gate: Albin, a childhood friend of Ulrich and I, and a thin Hungarian officer called Stefan Vancura, who would die with Mathias in Istanbul. They were the only other survivors of the Gate we would encounter, other than the Black Eagles we later fought and killed.

We had seen the last of Sergeant Horváth. An armourer called Siczynski showed us how to prepare the ammunition that was now our – and the Black Eagles' – only exit from this vale of tears. He was far pleasanter company than Horváth – quiet, soft-spoken and shy. He seemed quite gentle; ironic, given his profession. But this spiritual ancestor of our own Mr Veale was every inch the teacher that Horváth had been, if not a better one.

A week after recovery, Siczynski was satisfied that we could do our jobs. A day later he was gone, and I heard he went to the newly-formed state of Poland and pledged his allegiance to Marshal Piłsudski. He died in the Second World War; he was Jewish on one side of his family, it seems, and the Nazis swept him up.

And the rest of us? We who walked the Gate and survived became the *Falkenjaeger* – literally, the Hawk-hunters. (I suppose *Adlerjaeger* – Eagle-hunters – would have been more accurate, but somehow it doesn't have quite the same ring, does it?)

We established lines of communication as we'd been taught – dead drops, phone numbers where we could leave or collect messages for one another – and went out in search of the Black Eagles.

Colonel Ronge and the *Evidenzbureau* had already ensured that there was materiel and false papers in every territory they could reach, together with caches of gems that could be converted into ready cash in any country, enabling a man or woman to carry a fortune's worth in a trouser pocket. That was what mattered most: by then regimes were falling like houses of cards across Europe and beyond. Civil war was raging in Russia and God alone knew who'd be left to rule it; as for our former Empire, or Germany… in such a world, papers could become worthless overnight, and guns were as plentiful as leaves in autumn.

The Soviet Union would soon turn Mongolia into a satellite state, civil wars and warlordism would grip China, and the Ottoman Empire too was falling apart, with territories breaking away and changing hands. And in all that chaos, the Black Eagles and the *Falkenjaeger* waged war, because, apparently, there hadn't already been carnage enough.

And little by little it's whittled us down, my love; Black Eagles and *Falkenjaeger* both, until almost none remain. What a waste; what a stupid, wicked, pointless waste.

And the Gate itself is lost. But perhaps that's for the best, and not only because those who controlled the Gate used it as they did. I wonder, sometimes, how much the Emperor knew. Karl was a devout Catholic – the Church made a saint of him – and it's hard to imagine him colluding with what we saw in that chamber. I think of Josef and the rest, unravelled and screaming away eternity; I think of the inside-out thing that writhed out of the Gate. I remember how the things in the void entered and changed me, and wonder if that void might have been the Hell the Church taught me of as a child. And what, if I have gained physical immortality, I lost in the process.

So much story; so much to tell. But I want to tell it. I want you to know it all, to know all of me, and when I come home, you will. If you leave me, it won't be because of lies.

---

Dawn's breaking when I pull into our terraced street and park up in front of the house. It's that quiet hour when most of our neighbours, who work civilised hours, unlike me, are still safe abed and dreaming. When I switch off the engine, I'm struck by how silent it is. It takes me a few seconds to register that I can hear birds singing – the sound is very faint and far-off, but it's there.

I sit for nearly a minute listening to it. It's a very common, very ordinary sound; how many times must I have heard it by now? Or not heard it, because I wasn't paying attention? There is so much world out there, so much to see and do. Whole continents, as stated, that I haven't set foot on. So many things I haven't done, in all my century or more alive. And want to. Ideally, with you.

But that's to be talked about later. First of all, you need to know the truth.

I get out of the car and lock it. The Roth-Steyr's in my shoulder-bag; it bumps against my hip. I'll have to decide what to do with it. Perhaps it's finally time to throw it away. I unlock the front door and step inside, locking it behind me.

I know there's something wrong before I go past the door to the front room and see you in the chair with a blanket pulled up to your chin. You could have been sitting up, sleepless and worried, all through the night, of course. But I don't think you have been. I can tell somehow that you haven't. You don't respond when I stand in the doorway and call your name. And then I realise what's really wrong.

I can't hear you breathing.

I should run. I should run out of the house. No: I should run to your side, and try and help. But I do neither. I walk, instead, to your side. Because there's no rush. I already know there's no rush. It's over and done, whatever's happened here. And nothing else matters now.

You're sitting with your head bowed, looking down into your lap. From under the blanket, I can now see the ropes that lead around the back of the chair.

Strands of your hair stick to the cushioning behind you. To the dark stain, still not quite dry, on the fabric. There's a hole in the middle of it. I don't look at the back of your head. I put my fingers under your tiny chin and tilt your head up so I can see your face properly.

Your eyes are wide open. You look surprised. There's a small, neat hole in the middle of your forehead. Radiating out from it is a star-shaped pattern of smudged, grimy skin. Tiny powder burns, or as Mr

126

Veale would call them, tattooing, caused by firing a gun at contact range.

A silenced gun, I assume. So as not to wake the neighbours. So as to murder in silence – first you, then me. Which must mean that the killer is still here, close by.

But there's no guesswork involved, because I know someone's here in the living room. I haven't even looked, but I know they're sitting in the armchair opposite yours, on the other side of the fireplace. I can sense them. I can hear their breathing.

I should move. I should reach for my gun. But I don't. As before, there doesn't seem any point.

Who did this? But I know. I already know. Or at least, I've narrowed it down to one of two suspects. And I badly want to believe that it's Reeve, that it's Varga, because then I might be able to kill him before I die. Take him with me. One last thing. An ironic completion of the mission, long-delayed.

But there's a used cartridge case lying by your feet, as if left there as a message, just to let me know, and I can see as I reach for it that it isn't 8mm Roth-Steyr. I pick it up and check the headstamp on the base. Yes. What here in the UK or over in the US would be described as .32 ACP. Or, as we'd have said in the Empire, where we preferred the metric system, 7.65mm.

The same calibre as a Frommer Stop pistol.

"*Hallo, Bruder,*" I say at last.

I turn and look at him. He looks no different, of course. Except for superficial, surface stuff. His hair is in a man-bun, of all things – you would have joked that he needed shooting for that alone – and a rockabilly beard. My twin brother, the hipster.

He sits with one leg crossed neatly over the other. He wears corduroy trousers, a linen shirt, a waistcoat and a string tie, but everything is immaculately clean and pressed so flat that the creases have a military sharpness. One arm rests along the arm of the chair. The other hand, the gun hand, rests on his knee, and holds the gun that killed you. The Frommer Stop is an odd-looking thing – the breech and barrel form a thick, round tube, with a sort of rail running along the top. It always puts me in mind of an old-fashioned air pistol. Its barrel is extended by another long black tube – a silencer, which is now, of course, aimed at me.

"*Wie schön dich zu sehen, Schwester,*" he says at last.

I look up at him, and then gesture at you. I don't look at you. On the surface of things I feel terribly calm, but it's a thin calm, a brittle calm, like the ice that formed on the lake at Bradenstein in the winter of 1903.

I've always thought I'd ask Ulrich if he remembered that, should we meet again, but I don't. I no longer need to. Any hope that memory might heal the rift between us is extinguished by the sight of you in the chair. Actions speak louder than words.

"I should have let you drown," I tell Ulrich – still speaking German, like him. The wheel's come full circle, after all: we began as children of Austria, so let us end that way. I am the lake at Bradenstein: a brittle rime of pale glacial calm on the surface, a killing depth of black and searing water underneath. And like the lake at Bradenstein that day, I will kill him if I can. I remind myself that Ulrich only lived that day because of me, and I will not be there to save him now. Quite the reverse. I gesture towards you – I can't bring myself to look, in case that shatters the façade of my composure. "What about Varga? Shouldn't you be getting after him?"

"Already done," he says. "I'd been watching him. Careful. I knew he was good. I wasn't ending up like Erick and Tibor. And then I saw him with you."

"We recognised each other."

"And you let him live?"

"There was no point killing him. No point to it any more for either of us."

He snorts. "I knew where his car was, so I went back there. Picked the locks, got into the back. Then he got in, and then…" He imitates the sound of a gunshot.

I gesture to you again. "Why?" I say.

"I knew where you lived. We'd already spotted you. I saw you in the café. Drove myself over to lie in wait."

"No." I gesture, once more, to you. "Why? Why this?"

Ulrich shrugs. "Why not?"

"Why not?" I think my voice has risen slightly; I see Ulrich tense. I must be calm, give him no cause to start shooting yet. "That's the only reason you can give me?"

"You abandoned us," he says. "Left us on our own. All for what? Because suddenly you decided your vows didn't matter? Selfishness. And all to whore it with creatures like *that*." He gestures at you with the gun, and I almost jump at him, but the Frommer swings back towards me. "Just try," he says. "You took everything from me, sister. You left me alone with no-one."

"Don't be stupid, Ulrich – you had Tibor, you had Erick—"

"No-one! No-one I could talk to as I did you. You abandoned me," he says again. "All because I wasn't willing to throw it all aside – my sacred oath – so that I could… could… wallow in the mire with you."

He's grown censorious in his old age, even if his brow's still smooth and hair still titian; time was, he was as debauched as me, drank as many nights away and rioted with as many girls, if not more. But just as life among the fleshpots soured for me, it did for him, and he wanted something more. So did I, of course – I still do.

"That wasn't it," I sigh.

"Of course it was."

"I was tired of it, Ulrich. I told you at the time."

"You were bored."

"Tired. Weary. Sick of it."

"And you think I wasn't?" His knuckles are white on the pistol grip. "You don't just walk away from something because it's difficult or because you're *tired*. Or bored."

"I told you I wasn't bored." My voice is dead and flat. "Why should I explain myself to you, anyway? You've already made your mind up. I don't have to justify myself."

I'd like to, even so. I'd like to tell him that I understand, like him, that even if life is empty and meaningless, it's necessary to act as though it's not. We need some standards – of conduct, morality, belief, whatever – to cling to, to anchor ourselves against the mudslide of history, but the mudslide is never-ending and we must move with or against it. So we must shift the poles we anchor ourselves with, in order to climb. We can't just stay in one spot. And I've moved. I have stood for something ever since Berlin – for life, for healing, for compassion. I've tried to keep those flames alight. That's been my cause and I've stayed true to it. But none of that will mean anything to Ulrich, except as further evidence of my apostasy.

And maybe it's better that we don't talk. I'm already understanding my brother, my killer, too well. I'm starting to pity him now, and I mustn't, or I'll die. Not that the thought of no longer being here bothers me overmuch, but pain does – the process of dying and how bad he might make it for me.

"When was the last time you got laid?" I ask.

"You disgust me."

He thinks I'm offering to fuck him in exchange for my life. "Don't flatter yourself," I say. "I was just wondering. You know, to the nearest decade."

"I have a mission," he says. "No distractions."

I look over at you. "She never hurt anyone. She healed them. Saved lives—"

"Spare me the sob stories," he says. I think of Horváth, and the dog. If I feel any guilt, for anything I've done, it's that. "Desertion in a time of war is a capital offence."

"You killed her because I left you behind," I say. "Even though you could have come too." I can see my way out now, if I dare. "But you were too afraid."

His face is white, a muscle twitching in his cheek. "I was not afraid."

"Course you weren't, baby brother." But there's no point calling him that, not now. The little boy who fell through the frozen lake isn't there anymore, only this bitter, fanatical thing, steel-willed, closed-minded and stone-hearted. There's nothing left to reach. "Worse. You were a coward."

His eyes go wide and the gun comes up.

I throw my shoulder-bag at him; it's been half-hidden behind my body as we've gone back and forth, so I've been able to ease my hand inside and get hold of the pistol.

The bag hits him his face. He barely flinches, but it's enough to spoil his aim as I throw myself forward, and the bullet flies over me to thud into the chair, and I have the Roth-Steyr.

The shoulder-bag hits the floor. Ulrich's half out of the chair and his gun swings down towards me, but mine's already aimed. I see Ulrich's mouth open and then I fire, a single thundering blast. The bullet hits him in the throat and Ulrich falls back into the chair, gagging and choking.

I get up and go to him. He tries one last time to bring the Frommer to bear: I knock the silencer aside with a swipe of my free arm, then slam the Roth-Steyr down on his biceps. He groans and drops the pistol, staring up at me with terror and hatred as the lights go slowly down.

I'm tempted to let him die slowly, for what he did to you – but I know that isn't what you'd want. You wouldn't want any of it, I know, but you'd want this, now, to be over fast.

There are cushions on the sofa, so I take one. I'm expecting running footsteps and shouts, banging on the door, but there's nothing yet. Which means I have time. But not for this. I just want this over and done.

Do I feel sadness? Regret? Yes. But not for this man with the shattered throat. He's a stranger. I'm sad for my brother. I mourn him.

But he's gone.

And so I place the cushion over Ulrich's face, jam the Roth-Steyr into it, and pull the trigger again.

---

I stand by the window, waiting, but no-one comes. That single unmuffled shot might have woken the neighbours, but chances are they dismissed it and settled back down to sleep.

I put down the gun, untie your bonds, and lower you to the floor. Your skin's still warm; I only just missed you. Surely Ulrich would have had more pleasure out of killing you in front of me? But then, he knew I was dangerous. He just didn't realise how much.

I lie down next to you and hold your head to my breasts, stroking that matted hair.

"Listen," I tell you. "Listen. I've lied to you. I know I have. But that's finished now. I'm going to tell you the truth. I'm going to tell you everything."

And I do; I whisper the truth into your ear. You're the first one, ever, to hear my story, the only one other than me to know it all. I've seen nothing to suggest that there's any kind of afterlife, but I might be wrong. I hope so. I like to picture you still hovering nearby, not having yet moved on. If you are, lean close and listen up: this is for you.

Listen.

---

When I'm done, I lie there.

You're gone. Varga's gone too. Ulrich, Tibor, Erick: I'm all that's left.

Valerie Varden dies tonight. I have fake IDs; a little hair dye, and I'll be out of the country before anyone thinks to look.

And then?

I don't know.

Of course, that only matters if I choose to continue, and no law says I must. If I choose, I can die with Valerie Varden, and with you.

I only need put the gun in my mouth and fire. What then? Will the Papal Dispensation mean anything? Will our souls meet? Do I even still have one, or did I lose it in the void of the Sindelar Gate?

Questions, questions. But it would be so easy to end them all. All the questions, all the disquiet, all the memories of loss and pain. One squeeze of the trigger and I might be with you, wherever you are. Even if that's nowhere.

I can stop now. Withdraw from the game. If I want.

But I realise, as I stroke your hair, that I don't.

Is it a kind of strength, or something else I lost in the Gate? Perhaps I've simply lived too long. In any case, it seems as though love can no longer touch me so deeply that I can't live without it.

Though it shames me to admit it, I consider my possibilities – and there are so many of them. I could go to Australia, to the Americas. China. Japan. Or back to *Mitteleuropa*, to see Vienna again. A visit, perhaps, to Bradenstein, as well.

I'm sorry, my love, but I can't stay.

I lay you out, fold your hands upon your chest. I put pennies on your new-closed eyes. I kiss your wounded forehead; I stroke your matted hair.

And then I go upstairs, I shower and I dress; I pack my few requirements in a small backpack. They include the Roth-Steyr; it's the one constant left in my life, after all. And my ticket out of the game, should ever I change my mind.

One last kiss goodbye and then I'm away, with my backpack and my gun. The wind blows flecks of sleety rain, but I hardly even notice.

In so many ways, I'm used to the cold.

# Acknowledgements

My amazing partner in crime Cate Gardner let me read the entire first draft of *Roth-Steyr* to her aloud – well, apart from the scene we now call 'the dogocide'. Sorry about that, my love. (No dogs were harmed in the writing of this novella.)

Gary McMahon was the first reader of the finished work; thanks, mucker, for the kind words both in public and private.

My fascination with bizarre-looking early automatic pistol designs began when I read the late Ian V. Hogg's *The Complete Handgun: 1300 To The Present* at an impressionable age, and Ian McCollum's always-interesting YouTube channel *Forgotten Weapons* provided a lot of background on the mechanics and performance of the Roth-Steyr and similar pistols of its time. (No-one but me should be blamed for the song Valerie makes up about them, although I'd love to hear Julie Andrews sing it.)

For insights into the world of the Habsburg Monarchy, its final collapse and the chaotic aftermath thereof, *Twilight Of Empire: The Tragedy At Mayerling And The End Of The Habsburgs* by Greg King and Penny Wilson, *Ring Of Steel: Germany And Austria-*

*Hungary At War, 1914-1918* by Alexander Watson, and in particular *The Vanquished: Why The First World War Failed To End, 1917-1923* by Robert Gerwarth, were invaluable. Whatever I've got right in terms of history, setting or period detail is largely thanks to these authors; any mistakes are mine.

Grateful thanks are also due to Paul St. John Mackintosh, both for recommending the Watson book and for his advice on Hungarian insults.

Finally, huge gratitude to Steve Shaw, the gentle giant behind Black Shuck Books, for taking a punt on this decidedly strange tale.

I can't shake a nagging feeling that there's someone who helped me out on this that I've forgotten to thank; if I have, I'm sorry, and I'm grateful for the help you gave me.

Simon Bestwick was born in Wolverhampton, bred in Manchester, and now lives on the Wirral while pining for Wales. He is the author of six novels, the novellas *Breakwater* and *Angels of the Silences*, four full-length short story collections and two miniature ones. His short fiction has appeared in *Black Static*, *The Devil and the Deep* and *The London Reader* and has been reprinted in *Best Horror of the Year*, *Best of the Best Horror of the Year* and *Best British Fantasy 2013*. Four times shortlisted for the British Fantasy Award, he is married to long-suffering fellow author Cate Gardner. He's usually to be found trying to avoid reality and/or gainful employment, and (as many editors can testify) uses far too many semicolons.

# THE THREE BOOKS
## *by*
## Paul StJohn Mackintosh

*"I've been told that this is the most elegant thing I've ever written. I can't think how such a dark brew of motifs came together to create that effect. But there's unassuaged longing and nostalgia in here, interwoven with the horror, as well as an unflagging drive towards the final consummation. I still feel more for the story's characters, whether love or loathing, than for any others I've created to date. Tragedy, urban legend, Gothic romance, warped fairy tale of New York: it's all there. And of course, most important of all is the seductive allure of writing and of books – and what that can lead some people to do.*

*You may not like my answer to the mystery of the third book. But I hope you stay to find out."*

Paul StJohn Mackintosh

*"Paul StJohn Mackintosh is one of those writers who just seems to quietly get on with the business of producing great fiction... it's an excellent showcase for his obvious talents. His writing, his imagination, his ability to lay out a well-paced and intricate story in only 100 pages is a great testament to his skills."*

—This is Horror

**blackshuckbooks.co.uk/signature**

# BLACK STAR, BLACK SUN
*by*
## Rich Hawkins

"Black Star, Black Sun *is my tribute to Lovecraft, Ramsey Campbell, and the haunted fields of Somerset, where I seemed to spend much of my childhood. It's a story about going home and finding horror there when something beyond human understanding begins to invade our reality. It encompasses broken dreams, old memories, lost loved ones and a fundamentally hostile universe. It's the last song of a dying world before it falls to the Black Star."*

*Rich Hawkins*

---·---

"Black Star, Black Sun *possesses a horror energy of sufficient intensity to make readers sit up straight. A descriptive force that shifts from the raw to the nuanced. A ferocious work of macabre imagination and one for readers of Conrad Williams and Gary McMahon."*
—Adam Nevill, author of *The Ritual*

*"Reading Hawkins' novella is like sitting in front of a guttering open fire. Its glimmerings captivate, hissing with irrepressible life, and then, just when you're most seduced by its warmth, it spits stinging embers your way. This is incendiary fiction. Read at arms' length."*
—Gary Fry, author of *Conjure House*

**blackshuckbooks.co.uk/signature**

Also from BLACK SHUCK *Signature*

# DEAD LEAVES
## *by*
## Andrew David Barker

"This book is my love letter to the horror genre. It is about what it means to be a horror fan; about how the genre can nurture an adolescent mind; how it can be a positive force in life.

This book is set during a time when horror films were vilified in the press and in parliament like never before. It is about how being a fan of so-called 'video nasties' made you, in the eyes of the nation, a freak, a weirdo, or worse, someone who could actually be a danger to society.

This book is partly autobiographical, set in a time when Britain seemed to be a war with itself. It is a working class story about hope. All writers, filmmakers, musicians, painters – artists of any kind –were first inspired to create their own work by the guiding light of another's. The first spark that sets them on their way.

This book is about that spark."

*Andrew David Barker*

"Whilst Thatcher colluded with the tabloids to distract the public... an urban quest for the ultimate video nasty was unfolding, before the forces of media madness and power drunk politicians destroyed the Holy Grail of gore!"

—Graham Humphreys, painter of *The Evil Dead* poster

**blackshuckbooks.co.uk/signature**

# THE FINITE
*by*
Kit Power

"The Finite *started as a dream; an image, really, on the edge of waking. My daughter and I, joining a stream of people walking past our house. We were marching together, and I saw that many of those behind us were sick, and struggling, and then I looked to the horizon and saw the mushroom cloud. I remember a wave of perfect horror and despair washing over me; the sure and certain knowledge that our march was doomed, as were we.*

*The image didn't make it into the story, but the feeling did. King instructs us to write about what scares us. In* The Finite, *I wrote about the worst thing I can imagine; my own childhood nightmare, resurrected and visited on my kid.*"

*Kit Power*

———•———

"The Finite *is* Where the Wind Blows *or* Threads *for the 21st century, played out on a tight scale by a father and his young daughter, which only serves to make it all the more heartbreaking.*"
—Priya Sharma, author of *Ormeshadow*

**blackshuckbooks.co.uk/signature**

# RICOCHET
## *by*
## Tim Dry

"*With* Ricochet *I wanted to break away from the traditional linear form of storytelling in a novella and instead create a series of seemingly unrelated vignettes. Like the inconsistent chaos of vivid dreams I chose to create stand-alone episodes that vary from being fearful to blackly humorous to the downright bizarre. It's a book that you can dip into at any point but there is an underlying cadence that will carry you along, albeit in a strangely seductive new way.*

*Prepare to encounter a diverse collection of characters. Amongst them are gangsters, dead rock stars, psychics, comic strip heroes and villains, asylum inmates, UFOs, occult nazis, parisian ghosts, decaying and depraved royalty and topping the bill a special guest appearance by the Devil himself.*"

*Tim Dry*

———•———

*Reads like the exquisite lovechild of William Burroughs and Philip K. Dick's fiction, with some Ballard thrown in for good measure. Wonderfully imaginative, darkly satirical – this is a must read!*

—Paul Kane, author of *Sleeper(s)* and *Ghosts*

**blackshuckbooks.co.uk/signature**

Lightning Source UK Ltd.
Milton Keynes UK
UKHW010842260122
397711UK00001B/27

9 781913 038571